THE LITTLE MERMAID

The Junior Novelization

randomhouse.com/kids
ISBN 978-0-7364-2983-2
Printed in the United States of America
10 9 8 7 6 5 4 3 2 1
First Edition

THE LITTLE
MERMAID

The Junior Novelization

Adapted by
Melissa Lagonegro

Random House 🏠 New York

Chapter 1

Dark gray clouds filled the vast sky as a large wooden ship plowed through the rough ocean. The bow featured a mermaid figurehead, and three massive sails stretched high above the deck. Waves crashed against the hull, but the strong winds and the boat's sheer power sent it gliding through the mighty sea.

Three sailors wearing tattered striped shirts and bandanas atop their heads pulled a huge net aboard. The net was overflowing with fish. As the sailors worked, they sang songs and told tales about mermaids living deep in the seas.

Prince Eric stood at the fore rail of the ship. His black hair and white collared shirt blew in the wind. He leaned over the railing, smiling from ear to ear, with his beloved dog, Max beside him. Like his owner, the large, shaggy white and gray dog enjoyed every second on the ship. His

1

pink tongue flapped and his black nose wriggled.

"Isn't this great?" said Eric with a sigh. "The salty sea air, the wind blowing in your face . . . perfect day to be at sea!"

Eric turned to his most trusted servant, Grimsby. Poor Grimsby was feeling the effects of the bumpy ride. He was very seasick. He hung over the side of the boat, green with nausea, trying to avoid soiling his long black coat and purple ruffled collar. But the ever-proper and loyal servant managed to respond to his exuberant superior.

"Um . . . yes, delightful," replied Grimsby.

"A fine strong wind and a following sea," began a sailor, tying down a sail. "King Triton must be in a friendly-type mood."

"King Triton?" asked Prince Eric curiously, joining in the work.

"Why, ruler of the merpeople, lad," added another sailor, tossing fish into barrels. "Thought every good sailor knew about him."

Grimsby managed to pull himself away from the railing and stumble toward Eric.

"Merpeople!" he exclaimed, holding his sensitive stomach. "Eric, pay no attention to this nautical nonsense."

"But it ain't nonsense," replied the sailor, waving a fish in his hand as he walked toward Grimsby. "It's the truth! I'm telling you, down in the depths of the ocean they live—"

The sailor's tale was interrupted by the flapping fish. It slipped out of the sailor's hand and smacked its tail across the man's face, then flew through the air and over the rail. The frightened fish splashed into the water and swam as fast as it could, leaving a trail of bubbles. When it was safely away from the ship, the little fish stopped swimming, looked back up at the surface, and sighed with relief. It was free, and it was home.

Chapter 2

The fish continued his swim deeper into the blue water. He moved smoothly through tall bunches of green seaweed. He passed colorful sea vegetation bobbing and blooming in the crystal clear water. He swam by a school of pink and orange striped fish coasting above the rocky ocean bottom. He weaved through a group of jellyfish with umbrella-like bodies and long, dangling tentacles. Then he scurried through a cavern dotted with moss-covered rocks and vibrant plants and emerged in more open waters. He was heading somewhere special.

Giant shadows fell on the fish as he skimmed the sea bottom. They were the shadows of giant blue whales. The family of whales glided overhead, dwarfing the little fish.

Another family then joined the fish on his swim. A mother, father, and son swam with speed and grace over the coral reef. They had human upper bodies and long, scaly fish tails that propelled them through the water. They were mermaids! Like the fish, they were heading somewhere special.

Soon the reef was filled with merpeople. Together they swam over the ledge of the reef and up toward a cavern. They entered the cavern and a bright light beckoned them from the other side. As they got closer, the light got brighter and its source was revealed.

A glittering palace sparkled in the distance. Dozens of merpeople swam to the tall, majestic towers. They entered the regal structure through a long passageway that led them to a massive underwater concert hall. Huge stone pillars ran from floor to ceiling. Layers of rock acted as seating. A glowing anemone hung from the ceiling, casting a spotlight on center stage.

The fish and merpeople took their seats. They were eager to see something spectacular.

Chapter 3

Ten red and pink long-snouted fish stood at attention in the arena. They used their noses to make loud trumpeting sounds. It was the call signifying the start of the concert.

An orange sea horse with a fancy collar appeared and cleared his throat. His job was to introduce the guest of honor.

"His Royal Highness, King Triton!" announced the sea horse with his head held high. Despite his tiny voice and body, he immediately gained the attention of the crowd.

The musical fanfare began, and the eyes of the audience were drawn to a cavern high within the concert hall. Three beautiful dolphins pulled a chariot made from an enormous shell. In it rode King Triton, the ruler of the merpeople. He had broad, strong shoulders and a muscular upper body. His mustache and long white beard flowed elegantly through the water. A golden crown sat on top of the long white hair on his head. The massive biceps in his arms bulged as he clutched the reins of his chariot in one hand and a large magical trident in the other. His golden glowing trident was the symbol of his royalty and unlimited power.

The dolphins pulled the chariot through the concert hall, circling the heads of the cheering audience. King Triton waved his trident. Beams of light exploded from the ceiling and filtered down onto the crowd.

"And presenting the distinguished court composer, Horatio Felonious Ignatius Crustaceous Sebastian!" continued the sea horse with enthusiasm.

Sebastian, a red crab, had written all the music for the concert and would conduct the orchestra. Two goldfish pulled his tiny snail-shell chariot. Sebastian proudly waved to the crowd and blew them kisses. He caught up to King Triton's chariot and rode next to him.

"I'm really looking forward to this performance, Sebastian," said King Triton. "I know you won't let me down."

"Oh-ho, Your Majesty," began a flattered Sebastian. "This will be the finest concert I have ever conducted."

The dolphins brought the king's chariot to rest on a high peak with the best view in the concert hall. As the dolphins swam away, Sebastian parked his chariot beside the king.

"Your daughters . . . ," continued a raving Sebastian. "They will be spectacular!"

"Yes, and especially my little Ariel," the king whispered. He didn't want anyone else to hear him favoring his youngest daughter. This would be Ariel's first solo, and he was eager to hear her sing.

"Yes, yes," said Sebastian as he put on a huge smile for the king. "She has the most beautiful voice." But as he turned his chariot away from the king and toward the stage, his smile disappeared.

"If only she'd show up for rehearsals once in a while," mumbled the disgruntled crab under his breath. He furrowed his brow and gritted his teeth, but the show had to go on.

The lights in the hall dimmed, and a spotlight focused on Sebastian. The members of the orchestra were warming up, but they stopped when their conductor reached the stage. Sebastian pulled out a book of sheet music and walked to the top of a rock podium. He put the book down and popped his head over the rock for all to see.

The orchestra of assorted fish sat below him, waiting for their cue. Sebastian tapped his baton three times on the side of the rock. The orchestra was completely focused on him. With a smile and a burst of energy, he began to conduct.

Orange and black striped fish blew into red shells shaped like horns. A purple fish played a big J-shaped shell that resembled a saxophone. Three green fish with floppy blue fins played silly sea violins. A giant blue octopus banged on sea drums. A small green frog crashed two seashells together like cymbals.

Sebastian feverishly waved his arms as the orchestra continued to play. A curtain made of hundreds of bubbles opened and three giant clamshells came into sight. In time with the music, each clamshell opened and revealed six singing mermaids. They were all daughters of King Triton: Aquata, Andrina, Arista, Attina, Adella, and Alana. The mermaids danced, spun, and sang in honor of their beloved father.

King Triton sat proudly with his arms crossed and watched his dear daughters. He smiled and nodded. The six mermaids performed perfectly as Sebastian waved his baton excitedly.

Another giant clamshell rose from the stage as the mermaid sisters surrounded it. Sebastian looked back eagerly at King Triton, who was awaiting the climax of the show.

He swayed to the beat and looked on with anticipation.

The giant clamshell slowly opened as the mermaids sang to present their youngest sister, Ariel. It was her musical debut! The audience was on the edge of their seats. Ariel was the highlight of the show.

The clamshell opened . . . but it was empty, except for a lone blue cushion! Ariel was not inside—and she was nowhere to be seen! The mermaid sisters gasped. Sebastian dropped his baton in shock. He hid his head with his claws and sheepishly peeked at the king.

King Triton, clutching his trident, rose from his seat. He was furious! He slowly shook his head while his eyes turned red with rage.

"Ariel!" bellowed the angry father.

Chapter 4

In a ship graveyard, dozens of massive sunken vessels lined the sea floor. Jagged ship parts stuck precariously out of the sand.

A young mermaid with bright red hair popped her head over a broken mast. Her long hair floated beautifully along with the underwater current. She was curious, intelligent, and very adventurous. The ship graveyard was the perfect place to find human treasures—and Ariel couldn't wait to explore.

"Ariel, wait for me!" called a gentle voice in the distance.

"Flounder, hurry up!" replied the little mermaid, calling her friend. She couldn't wait to collect little treasures from the old ships. She was fascinated by everything from the humans' world above the sea.

A small yellow fish with blue stripes and fins breathed heavily as he made his way to Ariel. He was tired when he finally joined his inquisitive friend.

"You know I can't swim that fast," said Flounder.

Ariel didn't seem to hear. "There it is!" She pointed to a desolate ship lodged in a rock at the bottom of the sea. "Isn't it fantastic?"

A light from high above fell on the sunken ship. It cast an eerie glow, but to Ariel it was beautiful and exciting.

"Yeah, sure, it's great," replied a sarcastic Flounder, shivering with fear. He was petrified and wanted no part of Ariel's latest adventure. "Oh, let's get out of here!" He shook his head and began to swim away.

"You're not getting cold fins now, are you?" asked Ariel, playfully pulling Flounder's fin. She flapped her beautiful green mermaid tail and darted toward the sunken ship. In one hand she held a small red bag. She used the other hand to drag Flounder along.

Flounder broke away from Ariel's grasp and stopped. He didn't want to seem like a coward. "Who, me? No way!" replied the frightened little fish, putting on a brave front. He apprehensively swam to catch up to Ariel, who was already halfway to the ominous ship.

"It's just . . . ah . . . it looked damp in there," stammered Flounder. "I . . . uh . . . think I might be coming down with something." He held his head, but Ariel kept going. "I got this cough," he continued with a hack.

Ariel grabbed the side of the ship. Eagerly, she looked through a small porthole.

"All right, I'm going inside," she said. She pulled her head away from the porthole and looked back at Flounder with a sly smile. "You can stay here and watch for sharks." And with that, she slipped through the porthole.

"Okay, yeah, you go. I'll stay . . . ," began Flounder, smiling and nodding in agreement—until he actually realized what his friend had said. "WHAT? SHARKS? ARIEL!"

Flounder swam into the porthole to follow the little mermaid, but he got stuck! He twisted and turned, trying to free himself.

"Ariel . . . I can't . . . ," said Flounder, struggling to get loose. "Ariel, HELP!"

Ariel, who was already far into the ship, turned to look at her friend. She giggled and swam back to the porthole.

"Oh, Flounder," said Ariel. She knew her friend was a bit of a scaredy-fish. She grabbed him by his fins and started to wriggle him free. Neither one of them noticed a large, dark shadow passing over the ship.

"Do you really think there might be sharks around here?" whispered Flounder.

"Don't be such a guppy," said Ariel, finally pulling him through the hole.

"I'm not a guppy," he replied, trying to be brave as he followed Ariel down into a lower level of the ship. He closed his eyes and began to mumble nervously.

"This was great. . . . I mean, I really love this," he jabbered, not paying attention to what was around him. "Excitement, adventure, danger lurking around every corner."

Suddenly, Flounder opened his eyes and found himself face to face with a human skeleton against a wall!

"AHHHHHH!" screamed the petrified fish. He jumped backward and smashed into a post. The ceiling of the ship collapsed and pieces of rotten wood came crashing down.

"Ariel!" yelled Flounder, swimming into the arms of the mermaid and knocking her down.

"Oh, are you okay?" asked a concerned Ariel, trying to console her friend. After a gentle hug, she let go of him. He was shivering with fear. His teeth were chattering and his eyes were wide with fright.

"Yeah, sure, no problem," he replied. "I'm okay." He

tried to seem tough and brave.

Ariel quickly turned her attention to something above her. She shushed Flounder and swam through a hole in the ceiling. Flounder took a minute to collect himself and once again followed his curious friend.

"Oh my gosh!" exclaimed Ariel, looking inside a dark room filled with debris. Her eyes glittered as she spotted a sparkling object on a block of wood in front of a broken window.

"Oh my gosh!" she repeated. "Have you ever seen anything so wonderful in your entire life?" She held the shiny silver object up and stared at it in awe. It had a long, thin handle with three prongs at one end. It was a fork, but Ariel had never seen anything like it before.

"Wow, cool," said Flounder. "But, uh, what is it?"

"How do I know?" replied Ariel. "But I bet Scuttle will." She put her new treasure in her bag.

As the two friends admired their find, the dark figure swam outside the ship again and passed by the window.

"What was that?" asked Flounder, looking out the window. "Did you hear something?"

But Ariel was distracted. Her eyes focused on a wooden object on a ledge. She swam to it and picked it up.

"Hmmm, I wonder what this one is," she said, staring at it intently. It was a smoking pipe. Ariel had no clue what it was—but she couldn't wait to find out!

Unlike Ariel, Flounder was still leery of their surroundings and was getting more and more nervous. He floated with his back to the window, and the large, dark figure emerged silently behind him.

"Ariel?" called Flounder fearfully.

"Flounder, will you relax?" responded Ariel from the other side of the room. She was still engrossed in her latest find. "Nothing is going to happen."

Flounder turned around and gasped. An enormous gray shark loomed over him with his jaws wide open. Huge sharp white teeth were ready to bite. Red eyes glared into the room. In an instant, the massive shark smashed through the window, snapping his gigantic jaws.

"Ahhhh, shark!" Flounder screamed frantically, swimming faster than ever before. "We're gonna die!"

Ariel whirled toward Flounder. Her excitement had turned to fear. The shark chased Flounder around the room, crashing into ceilings and floors, destroying everything in its path.

Flounder swam into Ariel's arms, ramming her up

against the wall. The shark charged toward them, chomping his teeth.

Ariel overturned a dresser to block the oncoming shark. Holding Flounder, she swam around the room, pushing barrels into the shark's path. They swam up to the next level of the ship, hoping to get away, but the shark was fast and smart. He burst through the floorboards with his mouth wide open. Flounder almost swam into the shark's mouth! He screamed, and the two friends changed direction. Ariel and Flounder swam as fast as they could, but the shark was relentless—and hungry. He chewed through the floorboards as he pursued them. Ariel and Flounder gained some distance, but Ariel's bag got stuck on a jagged piece of wood and fell from her hand.

The shark was coming quickly. Ariel managed to grab the bag seconds before he reached her. Flounder and Ariel continued to swim for their lives. They raced to get out of the ship but came to the same porthole that Flounder had gotten stuck in earlier.

"Oh no!" screamed Flounder. He wedged himself in the hole. Ariel pushed Flounder with all her might, and he shot out of the ship. She squeezed herself through the hole just before the shark appeared.

The shark didn't let a small porthole stop him. He smashed through the wall of the ship and chased Ariel and Flounder through the sea and around a broken ship mast. Flounder banged into the mast and dizzily dropped down, barely avoiding the shark's bite.

Ariel turned around and noticed Flounder plummeting toward a large anchor on the sea floor. She dropped her bag and raced after him. The shark followed. Ariel reached through the hole at the top of the anchor to grab Flounder.

Gritting his teeth, the shark charged. The little mermaid pulled Flounder through the anchor hole just as the shark crashed into it—and got stuck! The chase was over. Ariel reached for her bag of treasures and smiled. She had won.

Flounder got nose to nose with the shark. He had a burst of confidence. "You big bully!" he said, blowing a raspberry in the shark's face.

The shark snapped at Flounder. Flounder screamed even though the shark was wedged in place and couldn't hurt him. Ariel laughed and swam toward the surface.

"Flounder, you really are a guppy." She giggled.

"I am not!" said Flounder as he trailed behind his fast-swimming friend. With a bag full of human treasures, Ariel and Flounder were off to find their friend Scuttle.

The sun's rays provided a tunnel of light guiding them upward. The two friends swam higher and higher toward the surface—a place mermaids were forbidden to visit.

Chapter
5

The sun sparkled on the sea. The waves were calm in the light breeze. Puffy white clouds floated through the crisp blue sky. A large rock formation sat in the middle of the water. The rock was home to a quirky and kind seagull named Scuttle.

Scuttle was an expert in all things human—or so he and Ariel thought. He was Ariel's greatest advisor when it came to the human world, though his information was often flawed. But what he lacked in knowledge, he made up for in heart. His white fluffy feathers, goofy beaked grin, and silly demeanor made him harmless, even to fish.

Scuttle lounged in his nest on the rock. The nest was made of straw, branches, and old ship parts. He hummed a sea song while looking through a large telescope. He giggled and sang some more as he put the telescope on his head like a giant hat. He was happy, carefree, and, at times, clueless.

As he admired the sights of the ocean, Scuttle was startled by a voice calling his name.

"Scuttle!" called Ariel.

Scuttle fumbled with his telescope and looked through it.

"Whoa, mermaid off the port bow!" he yelled. Scuttle saw Ariel and Flounder waving at him through the telescope. They appeared to be very far away since he was looking through the telescope from the wrong end.

He yelled louder so Ariel could hear him. "Ariel! How ya doin', kid?" He moved the telescope away from his eye and was surprised to find Ariel right in front of his nose. She was much closer than he'd thought. "Whoa! What a swim!" said Scuttle.

Ariel greeted the silly bird with a smile and then quickly pulled her sack of human treasures out of the water.

"Scuttle, look what we found!" she said excitedly.

"Yeah, we were in a sunken ship," added Flounder. "And it was really creepy!" He curled his nose, furrowed his brow, and lifted his fins for dramatic effect.

Scuttle focused his attention on Ariel and her treasure bag. "Human stuff, huh?" he said. "Hey, lemme see!"

He grabbed an anchor from his nest and dropped

it a few feet to the rock below. His leg got caught on the anchor's rope, and he crashed down on the rock along with the anchor. He shook off his fall and ran toward Ariel's sack, stepping on Flounder's head along the way. Diving headfirst into the sack, he rummaged around and pulled out the fork. As he held it up to get a better look, he scratched his head.

"Look at this," said the screwy bird. "Now, this is special. This is very, very unusual!" His eyes widened and he clutched the fork with both wings.

Ariel leaned in closer. She could hardly contain herself. "What is it?" asked the eager mermaid.

Scuttle examined the fork. "It's a . . . dinglehopper!" he declared. "Humans use these little babies to straighten their hair out."

Scuttle demonstrated the dinglehopper to Ariel and Flounder by combing the stray feathers on top of his head. He then twirled his feathers like spaghetti.

"See, just a little twirl here and a yank there and . . . *VOILA!*" exclaimed the freshly groomed bird. The feathers on his head burst into a spiked mess. "Ya get an aesthetically pleasing configuration of hair that humans go nuts over!"

Scuttle handed Ariel back her treasure.

"A dinglehopper!" giggled Ariel, staring at her discovery.

"What about that one?" asked Flounder, pointing to the pipe sitting on the rock. Scuttle gently picked up the pipe and spun it around. He held it inches from his eyes for a complete examination.

"Ah, this . . . ," began Scuttle as he walked around the rock with the pipe, "I haven't seen in years!" He turned back to Ariel and Flounder with confidence and enthusiasm. "This is wonderful . . . a banded, bulbous snarfblatt!" Scuttle held the snarfblatt up to his friends' faces.

"Ooooooh!" replied Ariel and Flounder in unison.

"Now, the snarfblatt dates back to pre*hysterical* times, when humans used to sit around and stare at each other all day," continued Scuttle. He gazed deeply into Ariel's eyes. "It got very boring. So they invented this snarfblatt to make fine music. Allow me."

Scuttle took a deep breath and his cheeks filled with air. He blew into the snarfblatt to demonstrate its musical usage. No sound came out; only a heap of sand, water, and sea plants.

Ariel flinched. "Music!" she exclaimed. "The concert! Oh my gosh!" Ariel frantically picked up the dinglehopper and shoved it back into her bag. "My father's gonna kill me!"

"The concert was today?" asked a worried Flounder, holding his fins to his face.

Meanwhile, Scuttle was coughing and fidgeting with the malfunctioning snarfblatt. He tapped it and took a closer look. "Maybe you can make a little planter out of it or something," he suggested.

Ariel snatched the snarfblatt from Scuttle. "I'm sorry, I gotta go!" she said, swimming away. She and Flounder stopped and turned back to Scuttle before diving down into the sea. "Thank you, Scuttle!" she called with a wave.

"Anytime, sweetie!" replied Scuttle. "Anytime!"

Flotsam and Jetsam, two sly and evil moray eels, lurked in an underwater cave nearby. The eels were the minions of Ursula the sea witch. Through their eyes, Ursula was able to see what went on in the ocean in her crystal ball. And at that very moment, she was watching Ariel and her little friend Flounder.

Chapter 6

Ursula sat curled up in a small, dark hollow inside her cavernous home. She was intrigued when her crystal ball began to glow with the image of Ariel and Flounder.

"Yes, hurry home, Princess!" said the brutish witch. "We wouldn't want to miss old Daddy's celebration, now, would we?" She grunted in disgust. "Celebration indeed, ha!" she continued sarcastically. "In my day we had fantastical feasts when I lived in the palace."

She reached a hand toward a small open clamshell. Four terrified shrimp sat curled next to each other as they prepared to face their demise. Ursula picked up one of the shrimp and popped it into her mouth.

"And now look at me," she went on. "Wasted away to practically nothing, banished and exiled and practically starving. While he and his flimsy fish folk celebrate!" She slid out of her dark hollow and down to the ocean floor.

The sea witch had the lower body of an octopus with long black tentacles and the upper body of a large woman with a big belly and two fat arms. Her skin had a purplish tone and her fingernails were long and red. She had evil, soul-piercing eyes and a shock of white hair that stood up on her head. Dark red lipstick coated the lips on her full face, and a large mole sat above her chin. She was manipulative and power-hungry, and she would do anything to get her way.

Ursula angrily paced back and forth as the image of Ariel and Flounder continued to glow in the crystal ball. "Well, I'll give 'em something to celebrate soon enough!" declared the sea witch. She abruptly turned toward Flotsam and Jetsam, who had returned from spying.

"Flotsam, Jetsam!" she yelled. The startled eels banged their heads on a rock as they jumped in response to Ursula's shout. They slid out of their hiding places to listen closely to their master.

"I want you to keep an extra-close watch on this pretty little daughter of Triton's. She may be the key to his undoing," said the evil sea witch. She was jealous of King Triton and his reign over the kingdom.

Ursula clasped her hands together and twiddled her fingers. Her long tentacles began to swirl around her face. Her eyes narrowed. She wanted to rule the ocean and overthrow King Triton—and Ariel would be the tool to make that happen. Cackling, she began to devise a plan.

Chapter
7

King Triton sat tall on his massive throne. A sheepish and guilty Ariel stood next to him, hanging her head in shame. Flounder looked on from a distance with a sad and equally guilty face as he listened to the king yell at his friend.

"I just don't know what we're going to do with you, young lady!" shouted the annoyed father.

"Daddy, I'm sorry. I just forgot," replied Ariel.

Sebastian, who was upset about his ruined concert, paced across the top of the king's crown.

"As a result of your careless behavior—" began the king.

"Careless and reckless behavior!" interrupted Sebastian. He stopped pacing and scowled down at Ariel.

"—the entire celebration was—" continued the king.

"Well, it was ruined, that's all!" interrupted Sebastian again. "Completely destroyed!" Sebastian jumped off the crown and charged Ariel. "This concert was to be the pinnacle of my distinguished career!" he shouted. "Now, thanks to you, I'm the laughingstock of the entire kingdom!" he huffed and puffed.

Flounder couldn't stay quiet any longer. He hated seeing his friend reprimanded. He stormed toward the throne and confronted Sebastian.

"It wasn't her fault!" the fish declared. But his confidence quickly faded when he made eye contact with the very angry king. He tried to hide his fear and began to act out their adventure while talking.

"Ah . . . well, first this shark chased us . . . yeah, yeah, and we tried to but we couldn't . . . and grrrr, and we, whoa," mumbled Flounder.

Triton and Sebastian skeptically looked at each other and then at Flounder. They weren't interested in what he had to say.

"Ah, I knew we were safe, then the seagull came and it was this is this and that is that," continued Flounder as he tried to act out Scuttle's silliness. Finally, he caught King Triton's attention.

"The seagull?" echoed the king, raising his eyebrows.

Flounder realized he had said too much. He covered his mouth with his fins, darted behind Ariel, and peered through her hair.

Ariel glared at Flounder. He had just revealed that they were up at the surface . . . where her father had forbidden her to go.

King Triton rose from his throne. "You went up to the surface again, didn't you?" he roared. "Didn't you?"

"Nothing happened," replied Ariel, trying to shrug it off.

"Ariel, how many times must we go through this?" said the king, holding his head in despair. "You could have been seen by one of those barbarians . . . by one of those humans!"

"Daddy, they're not barbarians!" Ariel protested.

"They're dangerous!" yelled Triton, throwing his hands up. His anger turned to concern and he approached Ariel. He gently put his hand under her chin and lifted it to make eye contact with her. "Do you think I want to see my youngest daughter snared by some fish eater's hook?"

Ariel quickly pulled away. "I'm sixteen years old!" she yelled. "I'm not a child anymore!"

"Don't you take that tone of voice with me, young lady!" shouted the king, pointing his finger. Ariel tried to get another word in, but her father continued forcefully, "As long as you live under my ocean, you'll obey my rules!"

"But if you'd just listen!" she pleaded.

"Not another word!" yelled Triton as he turned away. He was fuming! He looked back at Ariel for one last rant. "And I am never to hear of you going to the surface again! Is that clear?"

Ariel stared at her father. This time she couldn't muster up any words in rebuttal. Her lips began to quiver and her eyes welled with tears. She stormed off, and Flounder trailed behind her.

King Triton sighed and sat back down on his throne, heavy-hearted. He clutched his trident and rested his head in his other hand. He felt terrible.

Sebastian sensed Triton's remorse and swam to his side. "Teenagers," he began with a huff. "They think they know everything. You give them an inch, they swim all over you." He shook his head.

King Triton looked to his little crab friend for comfort. "Do you . . . uh . . . think I was too hard on her?" he asked.

Sebastian put his claws behind his back. He was happy to declare his opinion.

"Definitely not!" he exclaimed. "Why, if Ariel was my daughter, I'd show her who was boss! None of this flitting to the surface and other such nonsense. No, sir!"

King Triton listened intently to the preaching crab and

suddenly had an idea. He rubbed his mustache with his hand as he thought, then smiled. Sebastian was too busy rambling to even notice.

"I'd keep her under tight control!" continued Sebastian.

"You're absolutely right, Sebastian," agreed King Triton happily, staring at the little crab.

"Of course!" concurred Sebastian with his claws folded on his chest. He puckered his lips and nodded.

"Ariel needs constant supervision," said the king.

"Constant!" agreed Sebastian.

"Someone to watch over her, to keep her out of trouble!" stated the king.

"All the time!" responded Sebastian. He unfolded his claws and stared at the king.

"And you are just the crab to do it!" declared Triton, poking Sebastian in the stomach.

Sebastian's eyes widened and he quieted immediately. He looked shocked and sank down into his tiny shell. King Triton smiled, pleased with his new plan. But poor Sebastian could only groan in disbelief. He knew there would be no way to talk the king out of this. *What have I gotten myself into?* he thought.

Chapter 8

Sebastian wasn't thrilled with his new job. He walked along the sea bottom mumbling to himself.

"How do I get myself into these situations?" he said, shaking his head. "I should be writing symphonies, not tagging along after some headstrong teenager!"

Suddenly, Ariel and Flounder caught his eye.

The two friends looked suspicious. Flounder handed Ariel a bag. They were definitely up to something. They looked around to make sure no one was watching them, then swam off.

Sebastian lay low on the sea floor so he couldn't be seen. "Hmm," said the curious crab. "What is that girl up to?" He took off after Ariel and Flounder. He was much smaller and had to swim much harder to keep up with them.

Ariel and Flounder kept swimming. Sebastian finally

stopped to catch his breath. He was exhausted, and panted uncontrollably. But when he climbed over a rock, he was fascinated by what he saw.

Ariel and Flounder were in front of a cave barricaded by a huge rock. Ariel used all her strength to lift the rock, revealing an opening into the cave. Once again, she looked around to make sure no one was nearby. Together, Ariel and Flounder slipped into the cave, and the rock began to lower behind them.

Sebastian mustered up all his energy and swam as quickly as he could toward the cave. He darted through a tiny crack just before the entrance was completely closed off. His little body got wedged between the rocks. With all his might, he tried to escape. He yanked on a small piece of seaweed in front of him, trying to pull himself free. Finally, he popped out and went flying across the cave. Sebastian landed hard, smacking his head on an hourglass on the sandy cave bottom.

He rubbed his sore head and looked up in amazement. His jaw dropped as he gasped in disbelief.

He was in a giant grotto filled with objects from the human world. Layers of rock acted as shelves. Each shelf housed dozens of objects: plates, vases, bottles, mirrors, and decorative pieces of art. A light from high above shone down and cast a beautiful glow on the objects. Many were polished, and glistened when struck by even a hint of light.

These objects had clearly been collected over a long period of time. As Sebastian's eyes took in the massive space, he spotted Ariel resting on a rock ledge. She looked sad. She spun her latest find, the dinglehopper, between her fingers.

Flounder hovered over Ariel.

"Ariel, are you okay?" he asked, concerned.

"If only I could make him understand," replied Ariel. She stared at the dinglehopper. "I just don't see things the way he does. I don't see how a world that made such wonderful things could be bad."

Sebastian hid and listened with a scowl.

Ariel swam around her grotto, admiring the beautiful human objects she had collected. She showed some of them to Flounder. To her, they were treasures, but she wasn't satisfied with just collecting them. Ariel wanted more. She wanted to be a part of the human world. She wanted to run along the beach, dance, and soak up the sun.

She sat back down and gazed toward the surface. The sunlight lit up her face, which once again was filled with sadness. She yearned to free herself from her strict father and from the water.

Suddenly, a mug fell from one of the shelves and broke into pieces. Sebastian flew out of the mug and landed on a jack-in-the-box, which popped open, sending him flying the other way. He grabbed onto a tablecloth with his claws and pulled it to the ground. The table's contents came crashing down on top of him.

The loud noises and falling objects frightened Flounder. He swam into a knight's helmet and hid.

Ariel turned toward the noise. "Sebastian!" she cried.

Sebastian, wrapped up in beads with a pipe in his mouth and a cup on his back, crash-landed on top of an accordion. He spit the pipe out and hopped off the accordion, shaking debris from his back.

"Ariel, what are you . . . How could you . . . ," yelled Sebastian, still struggling to free himself from the junk. "What is all this?" With a kick, he broke free from the beads still wrapped around his ankle.

Ariel stared at Sebastian and shrugged. She was embarrassed and tried to come up with a quick response.

"Its . . . uh . . . it's just my collection," she answered awkwardly. She twiddled her fingers, then ran them through her hair.

"Oh, I see, your *collection*," mocked Sebastian calmly

with his foot stuck in a thimble. He lifted the fishhook that was still wrapped around his body and held it up with a fake smile. He quickly changed his tone and began to scream as he threw the fishhook aside.

"If your father knew about this place, he'd—"

"You're not going to tell him, are you?" interrupted a nervous Flounder.

"Ah, please, Sebastian," begged Ariel. She clasped her hands together. "He would never understand."

"Ariel, you're under a lot of pressure down here," replied Sebastian. He finally untangled himself completely and took Ariel's hand. He started to walk away, pulling the little mermaid along with him. "Come with me. I'll take you home and get you something warm to drink."

The sunlight was briefly blocked. Something passed by on the surface and cast a dark shadow over the opening in the grotto.

Ariel was distracted. "What do you suppose . . . ?" she began, and curiously swam away.

"Ariel?" said Sebastian, realizing she wasn't following him. "ARIEL!"

Ariel swam out of the grotto's entrance and looked up. She saw the bottom of a large ship. She heard booming sounds and saw sprays of colorful lights. And then she swam faster toward the surface for a closer look.

She wasn't going to let this chance slip by.

Chapter 9

The little mermaid popped her head out of the water and moved her hair out of her face. Her jaw dropped as her eyes locked onto a wondrous sight. A large ship sailed across the sea under the glow of a full moon. Fireworks shot off the boat and into the air, filling the sky with pink, yellow, green, and blue bursts.

Ariel laughed. It was the most magical thing she'd ever seen. She was mesmerized!

Flounder and Sebastian made it to the surface and popped their heads above the water, too. Sebastian glared at Ariel.

"Ariel, what are you . . . ," he began, but the bright lights and booming sounds amazed even him. He turned toward the ship and gasped. He couldn't believe what he was seeing! He held his head with his claws. "Jumping jellyfish!" he yelled.

Ariel swam toward the ship, diving in and out of the water.

"Ariel, please!" yelled Sebastian. "Come back!"

Ariel made it to the ship and floated inches from its side. She pulled herself out of the water and climbed up the side of the ship to an open porthole. She heard wonderful music and watched sailors dance and clap. She had never seen so many humans in her life!

A big, fuzzy, barking animal pranced around the ship's deck with his tongue out. He stopped and caught a whiff of an unfamiliar scent. He put his nose to the ground and sniffed his way over to the open porthole.

Ariel nervously let go of the porthole's edge and scooted to the side so she couldn't be seen. But when she peeked through again, the animal was waiting there with a goofy grin. He licked Ariel's face with his big slobbery tongue.

Suddenly, a voice called, "Max! Here, boy!"

Ariel rubbed the slobber off her face.

The furry animal ran back toward his master, wagging his tail. Ariel was still enthralled watching the silly fur ball frolic and jump.

"Hey, come on, mutt," said the man. "Whatcha doin'?"

Max jumped up on his master and licked his face.

"Good boy, good boy," said the man.

Ariel was completely captivated. The man's shiny black hair glistened and his dark blue eyes twinkled. She had never seen anyone or anything so beautiful in her entire life. She couldn't take her eyes off him.

Then she heard a familiar voice calling her and she snapped out of her trance.

"Hey there, sweetie!" yelled Scuttle, flying toward the ship. He stopped and hovered alongside the boat once he reached Ariel. "Quite a show, eh?"

"Scuttle, be quiet!" replied Ariel in a loud whisper. "They'll hear you!"

"Oh, I gotcha, I gotcha!" said Scuttle shifting his eyes back and forth, trying to be sneaky. He dropped down next to Ariel and peered through the porthole, hiding under her long red hair. He leaned in to whisper conspiratorially to Ariel, but he didn't have the ability to be discreet. His voice got loud and he raised his wing. "We're out to discover—"

Ariel quickly silenced the silly bird by holding his beak shut.

"I've never seen a human this close before," began Ariel. She rested her head on her hands as she leaned on the boat. She stared dreamily at the man, who was playing a flute and

41

dancing with Max. "Oh, he's very handsome isn't he?"

"Oh, I don't know," replied Scuttle, staring at Max, not the man. "Looks kind of hairy and slobbery to me." The seagull scratched his head in confusion.

"Not that one," said Ariel with a giggle. She grabbed Scuttle's face and directed it toward the man. "The one playing the snarfblatt."

At that moment, Grimsby broke up the festivities on board the ship and beckoned for everyone's attention.

"Silence! Silence!" he began. "It is now my honor and privilege to present our esteemed Prince Eric with a very special, very expensive, very large birthday present." He pointed to a gigantic mass on the ship covered with a tarp and an improvised bow.

"Ah, Grimsby, you old beanpole," said Eric, slapping him on the back gratefully. "You shouldn't have."

A very proper Grimsby stared back at Eric. "I know," he replied, rolling his eyes.

A sailor yanked the tarp off to reveal a huge statue of Prince Eric holding a sword and shield, ready for battle. Eric scrunched his nose at the sight of the tacky gift. Max wasn't impressed either, and growled at the statue.

"Gee, Grim," began Eric as he approached the statue for

a closer look. He rubbed his head, trying to think of a polite way to describe the gaudy present. "It's really something!"

Grimsby beamed with joy. "Yes I commissioned it myself," he said. "Of course, I had hoped it would be a wedding present, but—"

"C'mon, Grim, don't start!" interrupted Eric with a chuckle. He grabbed a telescope from Grimsby's hand and walked to the ship's railing.

Ariel and Scuttle ducked as Eric got close to them.

"Look, you're not still sore because I didn't fall for the princess of Glowerhaven, are you?" continued the prince. He tossed the telescope back to Grimsby.

"Oh, Eric, it isn't me alone," replied Grimsby. "The entire kingdom wants to see you happily settled down with the right girl."

"Oh, she's out there somewhere," said Eric, wistfully staring out to sea. "I just haven't found her yet."

Ariel smiled as she hid right below the rail where Eric was leaning. She thought of how wonderful it would be if she could be with him.

"Well, perhaps you haven't been looking hard enough," suggested Grimsby.

"Believe me, Grim, when I find her, I'll know," stated

Eric confidently. "Without a doubt!" He turned back toward Grimsby. "It'll just, BAM! Hit me! Like lightning!"

At that instant, lightning flashed and thunder boomed.

Chapter 10

$\mathcal{B}$olts of lightning lit up the sky, and thunder continued to crash. Raindrops began to fall, and the ocean started to swell. The boat rocked, and whipping winds sent the ropes flying.

"Hurricane a-coming!" shouted one of the sailors. "Stand fast, secure the rigging!"

Eric and the crew dashed about as the rain and winds increased. They tugged on ropes and fastened the sails as the ship bobbed up and down on the violent sea. Max ran around barking nervously.

In the ocean, Sebastian and Flounder got thrown about with the strong waves. Ariel and Scuttle clung to the side of the ship, but Scuttle was no match for the wind.

"OH!" shouted Scuttle. "The wind's all of a sudden on the move here. *Yeoooow!*" He lost his grip and blew through the air. "Ariel!"

A sailor struggled to steer, but he couldn't hold on to the wheel. The ship crashed through walls of water. Waves washed over the deck, sweeping sailors off their feet. Eric managed to grab the wheel, trying with all his might to control the ship.

Ariel lost her grip on a rope and dove back into the rough sea. She swam underneath the boat, then managed to reach the surface, where she saw a huge bolt of lightning strike one of the sails. It caught fire!

Eric and the crew looked up at the burning sail. But even more danger loomed. A giant rock sat in the middle of the sea—and they were headed right for it! Within seconds, the ship crashed, sending Grimsby, Eric, and dozens of sailors overboard. Grimsby saw the statue of Eric sinking into the sea. He tried to grab it, but Eric grabbed him instead and pulled him into a lifeboat.

Suddenly, Eric heard barking. Max was still on the ship, and he was surrounded by flames! Eric jumped off the lifeboat and swam toward the burning ship. He climbed up the side and pulled himself over the railing just as a fiery mast broke in half and came crashing down. He jumped out of the way, but the mast broke through the deck, spreading flames below.

Eric spotted Max on an upper deck and called for him to jump. The frightened sheepdog leaped into his master's arms. Holding Max, Eric dashed through fallen debris and flames.

Just then, a floorboard broke and Eric's foot got stuck. Max was hurled overboard. A sailor pulled him into the lifeboat.

"Eric!" yelled Grimsby from the lifeboat.

Eric looked at the flames surrounding him. He was helpless. The fire spread toward kegs of gunpowder. Within seconds, the ship exploded! A cloud of dark smoke filled the already eerie sky. Grimsby, Max, and the sailors on the lifeboat gasped.

Ariel had been watching the disaster unfold. She darted through floating debris in search of Eric, hoping he was still alive. Just as she spotted him floating unconscious on a piece of wreckage, the water swelled, and he slid and plummeted beneath the surface.

Ariel dove down after him. She grabbed him and tugged with all her might, determined to save him. At last, she managed to pull him back up to the surface. With her arm wrapped around him, Ariel swam away from the burning ship in search of land.

Chapter 11

The storm had passed. A few rays of sun peeked through gray clouds in the sky. The sea was calm, and the surf lapped at the shore.

Prince Eric lay flat on his back on the beach. His clothes were torn, and he was still unconscious.

Ariel lay next to him on the dry sand. She stared at his limp body. Her long green mermaid tail skimmed the side of his leg while she held her hand to his heart.

Scuttle landed beside them and leaned over Eric.

"Is he . . . dead?" asked Ariel hesitantly.

Scuttle pried one of Eric's eyes open for a quick examination.

"It's hard to say," replied Scuttle, shaking his head. He ran down toward Eric's feet and lifted one foot to his ear as if he were listening to something. "Oh," he continued grimly, "I can't make out a heartbeat."

Suddenly, Ariel saw Eric moving. "No, look!" she said, perking up. "He's breathing!" She brushed a piece of hair away from his eye and gently turned his face toward hers. "He's so beautiful."

Ariel began to sing to Eric as she stroked his cheek.

At that moment, Sebastian and Flounder washed up into a nearby tide pool. Sebastian saw Ariel caressing the human's face. His jaw dropped. He couldn't believe his eyes! Scuttle closed Sebastian's mouth as he happily watched Ariel sing to Eric.

Ariel's melodic voice and soothing touch awakened the shipwrecked prince. The clouds began to part, and a huge ray of sun broke through, shining directly on Ariel's head.

Eric reached for Ariel's hand as his eyelids began to flutter. When he opened his eyes, he smiled and saw a woman's silhouette against the sun. He couldn't make out many details, but the sound of her perfect voice was enough to reinvigorate him.

Just then, they heard barking in the distance. Max came running toward them. Ariel quickly pulled away and slipped back into the sea.

Max licked his master's face but jumped up when he heard a splash. He saw Ariel diving through the waves, and he barked and ran back and forth, trying to draw Eric's attention to her.

"Eric!" yelled Grimsby. He ran toward Eric and helped him up. "You really delight in these sadistic strains on my blood pressure," he said with a chuckle.

But Eric was too distracted to comment. Once he was on his feet, he started to walk toward the sea, almost in a trance. He was still wobbly and confused.

"A girl," began Eric, "rescued me. . . . She was singing. She had the most beautiful voice." Eric tried to recall his crazy experience, but he began to faint.

Grimsby reacted quickly and put Eric's arm around his neck.

"Ahhh . . . Eric, I think you swallowed a bit too much seawater. Off we go. Come on, Max." Grimsby and Eric walked farther inland. Max was frolicking in the water, looking for Ariel, but gave in and followed.

Ariel, Scuttle, Sebastian, and Flounder watched everything from behind a rock in a nearby tide pool.

"We just gonna forget this whole thing ever happened," began Sebastian, sitting on top of Flounder's head. "The sea king will never know. You won't tell him." He looked down at Flounder, who looked back up at him, nodding in agreement. "I won't tell him," continued the nervous crab. "I will stay in one piece." Sebastian clasped his claws and looked up at the sky.

Ariel paid no attention to Sebastian. She was fixated on Eric. She climbed on top of the rock and continued to sing. She knew in her heart that one day she would be a part of his world.

As Ariel watched Eric walk away, she had no idea that she was being watched in turn.

Flotsam and Jetsam lurked nearby.

Through her evil minions' eyes, Ursula had a perfect view of the pining mermaid in her crystal ball. "Oh no, no, no! I can't stand it," cackled the sea witch. "It's too easy! The child is in love with a human! And not just any human, a prince! Her dad will love that."

She looked toward a dark tunnel she referred to as her garden. Inside lived hundreds of miserable wormlike creatures that had once been mermaids. Ursula had used her evil magic to turn the mermaids into sad, hideous slugs.

"King Triton's headstrong, lovesick girl would make such a charming addition to my little garden," she declared.

The creatures shook and cowered as Ursula's shadow passed over them. Her wicked belly laugh echoed through her cavernous home. She was ready to set her plan to destroy Ariel and King Triton in motion.

Chapter 12

Back in the palace, Ariel's sisters sat at their seashell vanities doing their hair.

"Ariel, dear!" called Andrina. "Time to come out. You've been in there all morning."

Ariel exited an underwater washroom through seaweed curtains. She was happily humming and fluffing her hair. She swam to her vanity and looked in the mirror. She grabbed a big pink sea flower and breathed in its beautiful scent. She was oblivious to everything around her.

Ariel's sisters watched her curiously.

"What is with her lately?" asked Aquata.

Still humming, Ariel swam away smiling and holding the flower. Her mind was clearly elsewhere when she bumped into her father.

"Oh!" gasped Ariel. She smiled up at King Triton and put the flower behind his ear. "Morning, Daddy."

King Triton watched Ariel leave. The sisters joined him, and they all looked on as Ariel spun and danced down the corridor.

"She's got it bad," said Andrina.

"What?" asked Triton. "What has she got?"

"Isn't it obvious, Daddy?" replied Aquata. "Ariel's in love."

"Ariel . . . in love?" King Triton took the flower from behind his ear, smiled, and stared at it quizzically.

Meanwhile, Sebastian paced back and forth on a ledge at the base of a rock. He was clearly panicking. He had no idea how he would handle the king if he ever found out about Ariel's trip to the surface.

"So far, so good," said the nervous crab. "I don't think the king knows, but it will not be easy keeping something like this a secret for long."

As Sebastian worried and paced, Ariel rested on the rock above him. She dreamily plucked petals from a flower growing out of the rock.

"He loves me," she said, pulling off a petal. "He loves me not." One petal was left, and Ariel plucked it delightedly.

"He loves me!" Ariel giggled and rolled onto her back, happily holding the petal to her heart. "I knew it!"

Sebastian watched Ariel in disgust. He marched up the ledge. "Ariel, stop talking crazy!" he demanded.

Ariel sat up suddenly. "I've got to see him again . . . tonight!" she exclaimed. "Scuttle knows where he lives." She started to swim away.

"Ariel, please!" begged Sebastian, and grabbed her tail. "Will you get your head out of the clouds and back in the water where it belongs!"

"I'll swim up to his castle," began Ariel as she swam around conjuring up a plan. "Then Flounder will splash around to get his attention and—"

"Down here is your home!" Sebastian interrupted the rambling mermaid. He positioned himself right in front of her face and raised his claws. "Ariel, listen to me. The human world . . . it's a mess! Life under the sea is better then anything they got up there!" He directed Ariel to a rock. She sat down but didn't pay any attention to his ranting.

Sebastian continued to rave about the benefits of living under the sea. He enlisted the help of fellow crustaceans and fish to get his point across. He was so consumed in his own preaching that he didn't notice Flounder's arrival.

Flounder swam to Ariel and whispered in her ear. She hopped off the rock and swam away with him.

When Sebastian was finally done boasting about life under the sea, he looked toward the rock where Ariel had been sitting. She was gone.

"Ariel?" said Sebastian, confused and dejected. "Oh, somebody's got to nail that girl's fins to the floor!"

Suddenly, a voice called for Sebastian in the distance. The crab perked up and turned to find the king's royal sea horse messenger.

"Sebastian, I've been looking all over for you," said the messenger, panting. "I've got an urgent message from the sea king!"

"The sea king?" asked a nervous Sebastian.

"He wants to see you right away," continued the messenger. "Something about Ariel."

Sebastian's little legs buckled and his teeth started to chatter. He panicked.

"He knows!"

Chapter 13

King Triton sat on his throne, holding the flower Ariel had given him. He giggled excitedly at the idea of his daughter being in love.

"Oh, who could the lucky merman be?" he said, smiling at the flower.

Sebastian slowly made his way into the king's chamber. He was convinced that Triton knew about Ariel's trip to the surface, and he feared for his job—and his life.

Triton caught a glimpse of Sebastian approaching. He quickly hid the flower behind his back and cleared his throat. He was always dignified and proper in the presence of his subjects.

"Come in, Sebastian," called King Triton.

Sebastian gave himself a pep talk before talking to the king. "I mustn't overreact," he said. "I must remain calm."

He took a deep breath and walked toward the throne.

"Yes, Your Majesty?" he said, his voice cracking.

"Sebastian, I'm concerned about Ariel," began the king in a very serious tone. "Have you noticed she's been acting peculiar lately?"

"Oh, huh . . . peculiar?"

"You know, daydreaming, singing to herself," said Triton, peering slyly at Sebastian. "You haven't noticed, huh?"

"Well . . . I . . . uh . . . ," mumbled Sebastian, avoiding eye contact.

The king became more stern and gestured to Sebastian to come closer.

"I know you've been keeping something from me," he said ominously.

"Keeping something?" replied Sebastian with a gulp.

"About Ariel," said Triton, raising his eyebrows.

"Ariel?" asked Sebastian. He tried to stop his legs from shaking with fear.

"In love?" responded Triton, face to face with the petrified crab.

Sebastian cracked. He grabbed the king's beard and fell to his knees, pleading for forgiveness.

"I tried to stop her! She wouldn't listen! I told her to stay away from humans! They are bad, they are trouble." The little crab sobbed.

"Humans!" hollered Triton, jumping up from his throne. "What about humans?" His fury began to rise.

Sebastian suddenly realized that the king didn't know anything about Ariel's encounter with a human. He grinned guiltily and gently patted Triton's beard.

"Humans?" replied Sebastian. "Who said anything about humans?" He slowly pulled away from Triton and threw his claws up in the air.

Triton snatched Sebastian and clutched him in his giant hand. The look on his face told Sebastian that he wanted the whole story. Sebastian gulped and started to talk.

Chapter 14

Flounder led Ariel back to her secret grotto. They moved the giant rock at the entrance and slipped in.

"Flounder, why can't you just tell me what this is all about?" asked Ariel excitedly.

"You'll see," said Flounder. "It's a surprise!" He led her into the grotto.

Ariel froze when she saw her surprise. Her jaw dropped in amazement.

There in the sand was the giant statue of Prince Eric that she had seen on his ship!

"Oh, Flounder, you're the best!" she exclaimed, spinning happily and giving Flounder a huge hug. She swam around the statue for a closer look.

"It looks just like him! It even has his eyes," declared the enthralled mermaid. She looked into the statue's eyes and pretended it was real. "Why, Eric. . . . Run away with you?

Ariel is a fun-loving, mischievous mermaid. She's curious about everything from the human world.

During a storm, Ariel saves a human from drowning. His name is Eric, and he's a prince!

When Ariel gazes at Prince Eric, it's love at first sight!

King Triton orders his daughter to stay away from humans.

Ursula the sea witch realizes that she can use Ariel in her evil plans.

Ursula offers to make Ariel human . . . for a price.

Ariel agrees to trade her voice for a chance to live in the human world with Prince Eric.

Flounder, Sebastian, and Scuttle can't believe Ariel has legs!

Ariel has just three days to make Prince Eric fall in love with her. If she fails, she will turn back into a mermaid.

Ursula disguises herself as a beautiful woman named Vanessa. Using Ariel's voice, she puts Prince Eric under her spell.

As Vanessa gets ready to marry Prince Eric, her secret is revealed in the mirror!

Scuttle tells Ariel and Sebastian that Vanessa is really Ursula the sea witch! Ariel's friends must help her stop the wedding.

King Triton confronts the evil sea witch!

After Ursula has been defeated, Ariel and Prince Eric get married and live happily ever after!

This is all so sudden!" She giggled and whirled with sheer joy.

She didn't see a figure glaring at her in the shadows. When she finally stopped laughing, she opened her eyes and gasped. King Triton was staring at his daughter—and he was furious!

"Daddy!" exclaimed Ariel. Flounder hid behind a treasure chest.

"I consider myself a reasonable merman," said the angry king, approaching Ariel. "I set certain rules, and I expect those rules to be obeyed."

"But, Daddy, I . . . ," Ariel protested. She was quickly silenced by her father's booming voice.

"Is it true you rescued a human from drowning?" he asked.

"Daddy, I had to!" she replied.

"Contact between the human world and the merworld is strictly forbidden," preached the king, waving his trident. "Ariel, you know that. Everyone knows that!"

"He would have died!" replied Ariel, protecting the statue with her body.

"One less human to worry about!" Triton yelled.

"You don't even know him!" she yelled back.

"Know him? I don't have to know him!" said the king. He was getting angrier at every comment. "They're all the same . . . spineless, savage, harpooning fish eaters, incapable of feeling!"

"Daddy, I love him!" shouted Ariel. She gasped and covered her mouth, then hid behind the statue.

Sebastian, who had been cowering in the background, gasped as well.

King Triton was stunned. "No! Have you lost your senses completely?" he replied, red with anger. "He's a human, you're a mermaid."

"I don't care," said Ariel, still hiding behind the statue.

"So help me, Ariel, I'm going to get through to you!" shouted the king, leaning over the statue. His trident began to glow, and he waved it in front of himself. "And if this is the only way, so be it!"

He pointed his trident around the grotto, sending bolts of light in all directions. A globe exploded, and a candelabra shattered. Dozens of objects burst into pieces.

Ariel gasped in terror and swam toward Triton to stop him. She quickly realized she had exposed the statue. Triton realized it, too, and aimed his trident at it. With a determined look on his face, he fired a jagged bolt of light at the statue, disintegrating it!

Sobbing, Ariel threw herself onto the rock where the statue had stood.

Triton turned to leave but gazed back at his tearful daughter. He hated to see his beloved Ariel so sad.

Sebastian and Flounder sat on a rock as Triton's shadow passed over them. When he was gone, they slowly approached Ariel, who was still sobbing with her head buried in her arms.

"Ariel . . . I . . . I . . . ," stuttered Sebastian. He felt responsible for what happened.

"Just go away," whispered Ariel.

Sebastian hung his head low and left Ariel alone. Flounder looked at Ariel sadly and then followed Sebastian.

Chapter
15

As Ariel continued to cry in her grotto, two figures moved above her head in the shadows. It was Flotsam and Jetsam. They swam over her again to get her attention.

"Poor child," said Flotsam.

"Poor sweet child," cooed Jetsam in an eerily similar voice. Ariel lifted her head and stared at the two eels circling her.

"She has a very serious problem," said Flotsam. "If only there was something we could do."

"But there is something," answered Jetsam. Their eyes glowed as they got closer to Ariel.

"Who are you?" she asked cautiously. She was frightened but curious.

"Don't be scared," said Flotsam.

"We represent someone who can help you," added Jetsam. "Someone who can make all your dreams come true." The two eels became intertwined and spoke as one. "Just imagine . . . you and your prince . . . together forever!"

Ariel looked confused. "I don't understand."

"Ursula has great powers," said Flotsam.

Ariel brought her hand to her heart. Now she really was frightened. "The sea witch?" she asked timidly. "Why, that's, uh . . . I couldn't possibly." She struggled to respond but then put up her guard. "No! Get out of here! Leave me alone!" She quickly turned her head away from the eels.

"Suit yourself. It was only a suggestion," said the eels. But as they swam off, Flotsam kicked the broken statue's face and it landed right beside Ariel. She held the broken piece and stared at the face of Prince Eric. She looked back up at the eels and called to them.

"Wait!" she said with a bit of hesitation.

"Yessssss?" asked the eels in unison with big creepy smiles spread across their faces. They knew the young mermaid would not be able to resist their evil offer.

Meanwhile, just outside the grotto, Sebastian and Flounder were discussing Triton's rampage.

"Poor Ariel," said Flounder, shaking his head.

"I didn't mean to tell," said Sebastian guiltily. He hadn't intended to get Ariel in trouble. "It was an accident."

Both Flounder and Sebastian noticed shadows passing over them. They looked up and saw Ariel swimming away with Flotsam and Jetsam.

"Ariel, where are you going?" asked Sebastian. "Ariel, what are you doing with this riffraff?"

"I'm going to see Ursula," declared Ariel. Determined, she swam faster.

"Ariel, no!" yelled Sebastian. He grabbed hold of her tail.

"Why don't you go tell my father?" she said, glaring back at him. "You're good at that."

Sebastian stopped. Flounder swam up beside him. For a moment, Sebastian was at a loss for words, but he quickly realized he had to stop Ariel.

"Come on," he said to Flounder, and they headed after the little mermaid.

Chapter 16

$\mathscr{A}$riel followed Flotsam and Jetsam through the water, past volcanoes and geysers. Ursula's home was dark, desolate, and very far from Ariel's home. They approached a large, skull-shaped cavern glowing from the inside. Its mouth was the entrance to Ursula's lair.

Ariel stopped and stared at the ominous sight. She hesitated, but when the eels encouraged her to follow them, she gulped and dove into the skull's mouth.

Ariel swam through a tunnel and passed hundreds of the wormlike figures that had once been merpeople. She was petrified. Just as she was nearing the end of the tunnel, one of the slugs grabbed her by the arm. She was horrified but managed to free herself from its grasp.

Then she heard the voice of the sea witch.

"Come in, come in, my child," began the sinister sea witch. "We mustn't lurk in doorways. It's rude."

Ariel slowly swam toward the voice and watched as Ursula descended from a hidden cave.

Ursula plopped herself in front of her vanity and fluffed her hair.

"You're here because you have a thing for this human," she began. "Not that I blame you—he is quite a catch, isn't he?" She cackled and stared at her reflection. "The solution to your problem is simple. The only way to get what you want is to become a human yourself." Ursula looked at Ariel in her mirror.

"Can you do that?" asked Ariel. She was scared, but the thought of becoming human was extremely appealing.

Ursula smiled wickedly. She turned toward Ariel with a cunning look in her eye.

"My dear sweet child, that's what I do," she replied. She swam toward Ariel and slithered around her. "It's what I live for," she continued. "To help unfortunate merfolk like yourself. Poor souls with no one else to turn to."

Ursula approached a cauldron. She used her magic to reveal two sad mermaids. She explained to Ariel that she helped miserable mermaids find happiness through her magic. However, if the mermaids couldn't pay, they were turned into the creatures in her garden.

"Now, here's the deal," said Ursula, pulling Ariel toward her cauldron. "I will make you a potion that will turn you into a human for three days. Got that? Three days."

Ariel and Ursula hovered over the cauldron as lights and smoke began to appear.

"Before the sun sets on the third day, you've got to get dear old princie to fall in love with you," said the witch.

An image of a heart and a crown rose from the cauldron. Ariel stared in amazement.

"That is, he's got to kiss you. Not just any kiss—the kiss of true love," continued Ursula.

Sebastian and Flounder arrived and cowered in the corner as they watched Ursula lure Ariel into her evil plan.

"If he does kiss you before the sun sets on the third day, you'll remain a human permanently," Ursula declared.

Ariel continued to stare at the cauldron. An image of a mermaid transformed into a human running on legs appeared. Ariel smiled and leaned in for a better look.

"But if he doesn't . . . ," Ursula went on, moving closer to Ariel, "you turn back into a mermaid . . . and you belong to me!"

The running girl quickly changed to a mermaid and got sucked back into the cauldron.

"No, Ariel!" screamed Sebastian. Flotsam and Jetsam quickly wrapped themselves around Sebastian and Flounder to silence them.

Ursula grabbed Ariel's face and turned it toward her own. She looked exceptionally wicked. "Have we got a deal?" she asked.

Ariel pondered the decision.

"If I became human, I'll never be with my father or sisters again," she said.

"That's right," replied Ursula, acting surprised. "But you'll have your man. Life's full of tough choices, isn't it?" She cackled and pranced around Ariel.

"Oh, and there is one more thing," she continued. "We haven't discussed the subject of payment. You can't get something for nothing, you know."

"But I don't have any—" began Ariel. Ursula quickly covered her mouth with a tentacle.

"I'm not asking much," she interrupted. "Just a token, really . . . a trifle. . . . You'd never even miss it." Ursula drew face to face with Ariel. She stuck a red pointy fingernail under Ariel's chin to make sure she was listening.

"What I want from you, dear, is . . . your voice!"

"My voice?" asked Ariel, grabbing her throat. She was

confused by such an odd request.

"You got it, sweet cakes," replied Ursula. "No more talking, singing, zip!"

"But without my voice, how can I—"

"You'll have your looks, your pretty face," interrupted Ursula again. She moved away from Ariel and shook her hips from side to side. "And don't underestimate the importance of body language. *Ha!*"

Ursula tried to convince Ariel that men on land didn't like women who talk a lot, though she knew that in truth, Eric had been mesmerized by Ariel's voice when he met her on land. Ursula's plan was to make it almost impossible for Ariel to win the prince's love.

The sea witch slithered around her room, opening cabinets and pulling out bottles. She threw the bottles into her cauldron and a brew began to bubble. She was concocting the magic spell to turn Ariel human.

An image of Prince Eric's face rose from the cauldron. Ariel smiled dreamily and leaned in to kiss him, but Ursula quickly made him disappear. With a wave of her hand, a glowing scroll appeared out of thin air. It was a contract stating their deal and terms of payment. A moment later, a fishbone pen appeared in front of Ariel's face. Ursula stared at her eagerly and rushed her to make a decision.

Ariel took a deep breath and thought. She wanted to be with Eric more than anything in the world, and this was her chance, no matter how questionable the situation. She grabbed the pen and signed her name to the magical contract.

Ursula quickly sucked the scroll into her evil hands. She laughed, and her eyes became wide and wicked. She had a valid signed contract, and she believed there was no way Ariel would be able to win Prince Eric's heart without her voice. The little mermaid would not be able to uphold her end of the bargain. Once Ariel was under Ursula's command, King Triton would come swimming to his daughter's rescue. Then Ursula would have her greatest enemy wrapped around her finger.

Ursula waved her hands around the cauldron and recited a spell. A whirlpool emerged and rose higher and higher, engulfing Ariel. Lights flashed. The little mermaid was stuck right in the middle of the electric cyclone.

"Now sing!" the witch commanded.

Ariel began to sing a beautiful melody. A light in her throat began to glow.

"Keep singing!" shouted Ursula. Magical smoke in

the shape of the sea witch's hands moved toward Ariel and grabbed the glowing light from her body. The light continued to sing the melody. Ariel held her throat and watched as her voice disappeared into a shell necklace hanging from Ursula's neck. Ursula held the shell excitedly and licked her teeth with delight. She cackled louder and louder.

Ariel was engulfed by a trail of smoke. Lights flashed and thunderous booms crashed. Her body thrashed about, and her tail was split into legs.

Sebastian and Flounder looked on in horror. Ariel was no longer a mermaid—she had become a human!

Ariel immediately began to sink and drown—she could no longer breathe underwater! Sebastian and Flounder raced to her rescue. They pulled her out of Ursula's lair and up to the surface as fast as they could.

Chapter 17

A beautiful castle sat at the foot of a hill by the water's edge. Turrets of different sizes stood tall, topped with flags waving in the breeze. The castle was home to Prince Eric.

Eric leaned up against a rock in the sand with Max by his side. He was playing a tune on his fife. It was the same tune he had heard when he was rescued.

"That voice," began Eric, kicking the sand. He started walking across the beach. "I can't get it out of my head. I've looked everywhere, Max. Where could she be?"

Meanwhile, a little way from the shore, Ariel rested her head on a rock in an inlet. She was exhausted. Sebastian and Flounder were equally tired from their rescue swim. Sebastian clambered onto a rock and collapsed.

Ariel groggily shifted her body. She immediately saw her knees poking up from the water. She excitedly raised her leg and smiled. She wiggled her toes and giggled happily.

Suddenly, she heard Scuttle's voice in the distance. The silly bird flew over Ariel.

"Well, look at what the catfish dragged in," said Scuttle, landing on Ariel's leg. "Look at ya! There's something different." Scuttle scratched his head, pondering. "Don't tell me . . . you've been using the dinglehopper, right?

Ariel shook her head no as Scuttle grabbed her foot. He still couldn't figure out what was different about her appearance. He made a few more guesses. Ariel rolled her eyes and shook her leg up and down. Scuttle was clueless.

Sebastian sat impatiently waiting for Scuttle to figure it out, but finally, he just couldn't wait any longer.

"She's got legs!" he shouted.

Scuttle hopped off Ariel's leg in shock.

"She traded her voice to the sea witch and got legs!" yelled Sebastian.

"I knew that," said Scuttle, pretending.

"Ariel's gotta make the prince fall in love with her, and he's gotta kiss her," began Flounder.

"She's only got three days!" added Sebastian.

Ariel tried to stand up. Her legs wobbled and her knees buckled. She lost her balance and fell into the water, splashing her friends.

"Just look at her!" yelled Sebastian. "On human legs!" Sebastian gasped and covered his face with his claws. He panicked and began to rant about what King Triton would do if he found out. "I'm gonna march myself straight home right now and tell him, just like I should've done the minute—"

But Ariel quickly scooped him up and held him in her hands. She shook her head, pleading for him not to tell her father. Her eyes became teary and her face long and sad. Sebastian looked at her and felt terrible. He knew the only thing that would make her happy was to be with the prince.

"All right, all right," he said. "I'll try to help you find that prince."

Ariel gave Sebastian a big kiss and placed him on the ground.

Scuttle started rummaging through items washed up on the shore.

"Now, Ariel, if ya wanna be human," he said, picking up an old cloth, "ya gotta dress like one."

With a little help from her friends, Ariel wrapped herself up in the cloth and used a tattered rope to tie it on.

Scuttle whistled and giggled. "You look great, kid," he said.

Ariel looked down at her makeshift outfit. She felt beautiful! She didn't know how ridiculous she really looked.

Eric and Max were still walking along the beach when Max picked up a scent. He became very excited and started barking. He immediately ran off in search of its source. Eric chased him, calling his name.

Ariel and her friends were startled by the barking. As Max came running toward Ariel, Flounder dove underwater, Scuttle flew off, and Sebastian hid in Ariel's pocket. Ariel hopped on top of a rock to try to avoid Max.

Prince Eric called for Max, and Max charged back toward him. The dog tried to lead him toward Ariel.

"Quiet, Max! What's gotten into you?" asked Eric. The prince finally lifted his head and his eyes locked onto Ariel. "Oh, oh, I see," said Eric. He walked toward Ariel, who was still perched on the rock. "Are you okay, miss?"

Ariel smiled and tried to fix her hair, longingly gazing into Eric's eyes. She couldn't believe it was really him.

Eric looked at Ariel. Her beautiful face triggered his memory. He wondered if this was the girl he had been searching for—the one with the amazing voice. "You seem very familiar to me," he said.

Ariel nodded excitedly.

"Have we met?" he asked.

Ariel nodded again and leaned closer to Eric. Max barked excitedly and jumped on his master. He knew Ariel was the one.

"We have met!" said Eric, grabbing Ariel's hands happily. "I knew it! You're the one . . . the one I've been looking for. . . . What's your name?"

Ariel tried to answer, but no sound came out of her mouth. She had completely forgotten that she had no voice. She clutched her throat and looked down at the ground, defeated.

"What's wrong?" asked Eric. "What is it?"

Ariel tapped her throat.

"You can't speak?" he asked again.

Ariel sadly shook her head.

"Oh," replied Eric. Disappointed, he pulled his hands away. "Then you couldn't be who I thought."

Ariel sighed but had an idea. She tried to use her hands to describe how she had rescued Eric. But she lost her balance and fell off the rock into his arms.

"Whoa, careful," said Eric, holding Ariel in his arms. They stared at each other and instantly made a connection. "You must've really been through something. Don't worry.

I'll help you."

Eric helped Ariel regain her balance and wrapped his arm around her shoulder. He led her toward his castle.

Ariel looked at Flounder and Scuttle, who were at the water's edge. She grinned from ear to ear. She was a step closer to making her dreams come true.

Chapter 18

Heaps of white soapy foam filled up a big bathtub. Ariel was covered with bubbles and happily popped them with her hands. She was fascinated by this new experience.

Carlotta, a kind and concerned housemaid, poured a cup of warm water over Ariel's head to rinse her hair.

"Washed up from a shipwreck," said Carlotta sympathetically. "Oh, you poor thing. We'll have you feeling better in no time." She picked up Ariel's tattered "dress" and looked at it in disgust.

Sebastian popped his head out of the pocket and gasped.

"I'll just . . . uh . . . get this washed for you," said Carlotta. She left the bathroom and threw the dress into a basin filled with soap and water.

Without any chance of escaping, Sebastian plunged into the water, too. Three other housemaids gossiped as they did the wash. Sebastian was still in the pocket and got scraped up and down a washboard. He hiccupped bubbles.

A housemaid then put the dress through a wringer to dry it. Sebastian popped through the other side, but not before he was squished and flattened. His hard shell creaked and cracked after taking quite a hit.

He was quickly scooped up in more fabric, which was then hung on a moving clothesline. Sebastian saw an open window and jumped through. He was tired and achy, and he closed his eyes and sighed with relief at his escape. But when he opened his eyes a moment later, he gasped in fear.

He was in the castle's kitchen. Knives lined the wall. There were fish boiling in pots and fish on the chopping block. Crabs were being stuffed on a platter right in front of his face. Sebastian was petrified! He fainted.

Meanwhile, in the grand dining room, Grimsby sat in a chair at the head of the long, elegant table. He was trying to convince Eric that women didn't swim around rescuing people from the ocean.

Eric believed otherwise. He gazed out the large windows. "I'm telling you, Grim, she was real," he began. "I'm gonna find that girl, and I'm gonna marry her."

The gentlemen were interrupted by a female voice.

"Come on, honey," said Carlotta, pulling Ariel into the room. "Don't be shy."

Ariel walked into a dark shadow of the regal dining room. Then she stepped into the light, and she seemed to glow with beauty. Her long red hair was pulled back into a side clip, revealing lovely drop earrings. A pink and white dress with puffed sleeves and a tiered ruffled skirt fit her perfectly. She looked stunning, and Eric couldn't help staring at her.

Ariel walked toward Eric with a huge smile. He was in awe of her.

"Oh, Eric, isn't she a vision," said Grimsby, who was equally taken with her beauty.

"You look wonderful," said Eric, who was almost at a loss for words.

Ariel beamed with happiness and didn't take her eyes off Eric.

Grimsby took Ariel's hand and escorted her to the table. "It's not often that we have such a lovely dinner guest," said Grimsby as he and Eric joined Ariel at the table.

Ariel noticed a dinglehopper on the table—though to everyone else it was just a fork. She confidently picked it up and began to comb her hair with it! Eric and Grimsby stared at Ariel quizzically. They couldn't imagine why in the world she would be combing her hair with a fork.

Ariel took a cue from their awkward stare and put the fork down. She was embarrassed but quickly perked up when she saw Grimsby use a match to light his pipe— though to her, it was a music-making snarfblatt.

She seemed very interested in the pipe, so Grimsby handed it to her. She grabbed it excitedly and blew into it. A huge puff of tobacco hit Grimsby in his face, turning it black.

Eric was very amused and laughed merrily.

"Why, Eric!" exclaimed Carlotta, putting her hand on his shoulder. "That's the first time I've seen you smile in weeks!"

Ariel, who was once again embarrassed, gazed up at Eric happily when she heard that news.

Grimsby wiped the tobacco off his nose with a handkerchief. He was not amused, but tried to regain his dignity and change the subject.

"Carlotta, my dear, what's for dinner?" he asked.

"Oh, you're going to love it!" she replied. "Chef's been fixing his specialty . . . stuffed crabs!"

Chapter 19

In the kitchen, Sebastian peeked out from behind a large canister. He was frightened, but he needed to find an escape route. Unfortunately, Louis, the chef, was going to make that escape quite tricky.

The plump French chef fumbled around the kitchen. A big red bow was wrapped around the collar of his white puffy-sleeved shirt. His chef's hat wobbled back and forth on top of his head, and his long, thin mustache curled up at the ends.

Louis took his job as a chef very seriously and found great pleasure in preparing his meals. He hummed a tune happily as he carried a huge bowl of dead fish to the counter. Sebastian winced and cowered behind the canister.

Louis loved to cook and eat fish—all kinds of fish, including crustaceans. He grabbed a huge cleaver from the counter and chopped off the head of a fish. He continued with the rest of the fish and then pulled out their bones.

Sebastian watched in horror and covered his mouth. He was sick to his stomach.

Louis tossed pieces of fish into a sizzling pan. He danced around the kitchen sautéing, stirring, and plating all different kinds of fish.

Sebastian had to get out of there—and quickly! He scurried across the counter, jumping with every crash of the cleaver. He hid under a piece of lettuce and used it as a disguise to move across a table. But before he could get away, Louis grabbed the lettuce to use in his cooking.

"I have missed one!" said Louis as he noticed a frozen Sebastian sitting under the lettuce leaf. He thought Sebastian was dead and happily tossed him into a pot of sauce. He threw flour on the crab's face and then stuffed breadcrumbs into his shell. Still singing, he threw Sebastian across the room toward a pot of boiling water.

Sebastian grabbed the side of the pot before hitting the water and jumped back onto the counter with a thud.

Louis turned to see where the noise had come from. When he spotted Sebastian on the counter, he picked him up with a big fork.

"What is this?" asked the curious chef, bringing

Sebastian close to his face.

Suddenly, Sebastian pinched Louis's nose with his claws.

Louis screamed, sending Sebastian flying through the air.

Chaos ensued as the angry chef chased the frantic crab around the kitchen. Pots and pans crashed to the floor, tables broke in half, and delicate crystal dinnerware shattered.

An enraged Louis chased Sebastian with knives and cleavers, but Sebastian managed to escape every time. Sebastian ran toward a huge cabinet filled with dishes and glassware. Louis charged after him, destroying every dish and glass.

The noise was so loud that Ariel, Eric, Grimsby, and Carlotta heard the racket from the dining room.

"I think I better go see what Louis is up to," said Carlotta nervously.

She entered the kitchen, which was in disarray. She found Louis digging through the rubble looking for something. She immediately yelled at him, grabbed a platter of covered dishes, and left the mess in a huff. She returned to the dining room and placed the dishes in front of Grimsby, Eric, and Ariel.

"You know, Eric," began Grimsby, "perhaps our young

guest might enjoy seeing some of the sights of the kingdom. Something in the way of a tour."

"Uh . . . I'm sorry, Grim, what was that?" asked Eric. He was distracted. He couldn't stop staring at Ariel.

Grimsby leaned in closer to Eric and lectured the prince about how he needed to get out more. As he talked, he lifted the cover off his dish.

Sebastian was sitting on the plate!

Ariel saw Sebastian and gasped. Sebastian shushed her nervously. Grimsby and Eric continued to talk as Ariel lifted the lid off her platter and waved Sebastian toward her. The quick crab scooted off Grimsby's plate and scurried across the table onto Ariel's plate without being seen. She replaced the lid, trapping Sebastian beneath it, and immediately returned her attention to Eric.

"Well, what do you say?" Eric said, looking back at Ariel. "Would you like to join me on a tour of my kingdom tomorrow?"

Ariel nodded enthusiastically.

"Wonderful!" exclaimed Grimsby. "Now let's eat before this crab wanders off my plate." Grimsby looked down at his empty plate. He was confused. His crab was missing— thankfully!

Chapter 20

That evening, Ariel peered out her bedroom window. She leaned on the railing and stared dreamily at the grass below, where Eric was playing with Max. Max licked Eric's face and Ariel giggled to herself.

Eric noticed Ariel watching him. He looked up at her, waved, and smiled. Ariel was embarrassed. She waved back and stepped away from the balcony, heading back into her room.

Eric found his new houseguest intriguing. He stared merrily at Ariel's window. There was something very special about her.

Ariel walked around her lavish room. Large pictures lined the walls. A plush rug covered the floor. An enormous bed with a beautiful canopy stood in the center of the room. She was was really looking forward to her outing with Eric in the morning.

She picked up a fork and brushed her hair with it, smiling innocently. Then she put it on her nightstand and patted Sebastian on his head.

"This has to be, without a doubt, the single most humiliating day of my life," grumbled a disgruntled Sebastian. "I hope that you appreciate what I go through for you, young lady."

Ariel paid no attention to Sebastian. She flopped down on her soft, fluffy bed. She was startled by the new feeling but quickly realized the bed was fun and comfortable. She bounced up and down and then nestled into her pillow.

"Now we got to make a plan to get that boy to kiss you," continued Sebastian. "Tomorrow, when he takes you for that ride, you gotta look your best."

He then batted his eyelashes and puckered his lips, trying to show Ariel how to win over the prince. Suddenly, he realized that Ariel was fast asleep. He shrugged and smiled at her. He walked over to a candle and blew it out, then hopped off the nightstand onto the bed. He moved Ariel's hair from her face and snuggled up next to her on a pillow. Like Ariel, Sebastian was very comfortable, and he, too, fell fast asleep.

Things weren't as comfortable in the sea. King Triton paced in his chamber and stared out a window to the open sea. A little messenger sea horse briskly swam toward the king. He had just returned from another search.

"Any sign of them?" asked the king.

"No, Your Majesty," replied the sea horse, shaking his head. "We've searched everywhere. We've found no trace of your daughter or Sebastian."

"Well, keep looking!" demanded the king. He was angry, but his tone began to soften. "Leave no shell unturned, no coral unexplored. Let no one in this kingdom sleep until she's safe at home!"

"Yes, sire!" said the sea horse obediently. He bowed and swam away.

King Triton sat back down on his throne, holding his head in despair.

He blamed himself for Ariel's disappearance.

"What've I done?" said the king, shaking his head. "What've I done?"

Chapter 21

It was a glorious morning on land. The guards opened the gates as Eric and Ariel set off for the city in a horse-drawn carriage.

Ariel, wearing a beautiful blue dress, was fascinated by everything she saw. She hung over the side of the carriage just to see the trotting of the horses' hooves.

A river ran along next to the road. Flounder jumped in and out of the water to see what was going on. He caught the attention of Sebastian, who was hiding beside Ariel in the carriage.

"Has he kissed her yet?" asked Flounder.

"Not yet!" whispered Sebastian.

Ariel and Eric rode into the village marketplace. They parked the carriage and strolled around. Ariel had never seen so many amazing things—crates of chirping chickens, a puppet show, and streets filled with busy shoppers. Her eyes were wide with excitement. She spotted a group of dancers and pulled Eric toward them. She took his hands and the two began to dance. They were both having so much fun! They truly enjoyed each other's company, despite Ariel's inability to speak. Her dreams were coming true!

They headed back to the carriage and continued their tour of the kingdom.

Scuttle flew overhead and saw Flounder in the river.

"Yo, Flounder!" yelled Scuttle. "Any kissing?"

"No, not yet," said Flounder, shaking his head.

"Well, they better get crackin'!" replied Scuttle.

Ariel and Eric left the village and rode toward a beautiful lagoon. The sun was beginning to set, and the sky turned a soft shade of purple. Wispy trees hung down over the lily pads. It was the perfect romantic setting.

Ariel and Eric took a boat ride. Eric slowly rowed across the calm water as Ariel took everything in.

Scuttle landed on a rock next to Flounder, who was floating in the lagoon.

"One day left and that boy ain't puckered up once!" said Scuttle. "This calls for a little vocal romantic stimulation!"

Scuttle flew up and landed on a high tree branch, scaring all the smaller birds away. He cleared his throat and began to hum a most unpleasant tune in a most unappealing voice.

Eric and Ariel rowed right beneath Scuttle's tree.

"Somebody should find that poor animal and put it out of its misery," said Eric, wrinkling his nose.

Ariel smiled at him, but she knew Scuttle was the one making the racket. She looked up at him in the tree. He gave her a big wink and continued to serenade them. Ariel winced and held her head in her hands.

Sebastian, who was in Ariel's pocket, popped up and covered his ears. He was equally disgusted by all the noise. He hopped off the back of the boat and swam underwater, where he grabbed a sea plant to use as a baton.

"You want something done, you've got to do it yourself," said Sebastian as he swam back up to the surface with his makeshift baton. Several ducks and turtles swam toward Sebastian, awaiting their cue.

"First you got to create the mood," continued Sebastian. He began to conduct. The ducks started playing percussion on the turtles' shells. Grasshoppers turned their bodies into string instruments. Wispy plants blew in the wind, creating a lovely sound. Sebastian formed an instant orchestra to create an atmosphere for falling in love.

He sat on a stem and sang into Eric's ear as the rowboat

floated by. Eric looked confused at first but quickly became more enthralled by Ariel. Sebastian's music was working! Ariel and Eric gazed deeper into each other's eyes.

"You know, I feel really bad not knowing your name," said Eric, rowing the boat. "Well, maybe I can guess." He leaned back and suggested a few different names. With each name, Ariel shook her head no.

Suddenly, Eric heard a voice and looked around quizzically.

"Ariel!" whispered Sebastian, hanging off the side of the boat. "Her name is Ariel!"

"Ariel?" said Eric, grabbing her hands.

Ariel nodded in agreement and looked longingly into Eric's eyes.

"Ariel. That's kind of pretty," said Eric, holding her hands gently.

They smiled at each other as the boat floated farther into the blue lagoon and drifted under a willow tree. Frogs, tadpoles, birds, and fish continued to serenade the couple as Sebastian led the chorus. Fireflies lit up the sky above them. More fish, including Flounder, blew water in the air around the boat, creating a magical fountain.

It was the perfect setting for their first kiss. Eric leaned toward Ariel and they both puckered their lips. They were about to kiss—but the moment was ruined in an instant. Without any warning, the boat flipped over!

Sebastian smacked his head with his claw in disbelief. He couldn't see that the sudden dunking was the work of Flotsam and Jetsam. The wicked eels cackled and hid behind the overturned boat. They had purposely tipped it over to prevent Ariel and Eric from kissing!

Chapter 22

In her crystal ball, Ursula watched the drenched Ariel and Eric get up after falling out of the boat. She was proud of Flotsam and Jetsam for a job well done.

"Nice work, boys," she said. "That was a close one—too close." She wandered over to her potion ingredients with a plan. "At this rate, he'll be kissing her by sunset for sure. Well, it's time Ursula took matters into her own tentacles."

She grabbed a few ingredients and threw them into the smoking cauldron. A magical potion began to brew.

"Triton's daughter will be mine!" exclaimed Ursula, clutching the shell necklace with Ariel's voice inside. "And then I'll make him writhe. . . . I'll see him wriggle like a worm on a hook!"

Lights flashed and smoke engulfed the evil sea witch. She began to laugh wildly, but her token deep and raspy cackle changed . . . and so did her body. She transformed into a young and beautiful woman!

Back on land, a full moon glowed in the sky over Eric's castle. A thick fog began to roll in as Eric played his fife on a balcony. He looked longingly out to sea while playing the tune sung to him by the mystery girl who had saved his life. He couldn't forget about her, though he had become quite interested in Ariel.

Grimsby walked to the balcony and put his hand on Eric's shoulder.

"If I may say," began Grimsby. "Far better than any dream girl is one of flesh and blood. One warm and caring—and right before your eyes." Grimsby pointed to Ariel's window as he walked away.

Eric looked in the window and saw Ariel brushing her hair. His eyes lit up and he smiled. He gazed down at his fife and back up at the window. Eric realized that Grimsby was right—Ariel was amazing. He threw the fife into the sea and started to walk into the castle.

Suddenly, Eric stopped. He heard a voice singing— the voice he had been longing for! He ran back out to the balcony and looked down toward the sea. He saw a young maiden walking along the sandy shore. She had long hair and was wearing a shell necklace. It was hard for him to see many details through the thick fog.

The girl's necklace began to glow.

A stream of light flowed out of the shell as the girl continued to sing. The light traveled up to the balcony and right into Eric's eyes as he stared down at the maiden. His eyes begin to glow, and he was immediately hypnotized. Prince Eric was under a spell. It was the work of Ursula's dark magic!

Chapter 23

The sun was shining as Scuttle glided through the sky. He was in a hurry and soared toward Ariel's window.

"Ariel!" called Scuttle. "Wake up! Wake up!" He flew through her window and landed on her bed. Ariel and Sebastian were still sound asleep. "I just heard the news!" he continued excitedly.

Ariel sat up groggily and Sebastian stretched.

"Congratulations, kiddo—we did it!" exclaimed Scuttle, shaking Ariel's hand wildly. He wrapped his wings around Ariel and Sebastian. "The whole town's buzzing about the prince getting himself hitched this afternoon! You know, he's getting married! I just wanna wish you luck! Catch ya later. I wouldn't miss it!" shouted the silly bird as he flew back out the window.

Ariel was a bit confused. Could Scuttle possibly be talking about a marriage between her and Eric? A huge smile spread across her face, and she jumped out of bed. She picked up Sebastian and spun around happily. Sebastian stared at her, dumbfounded, as she kissed him on the cheek and placed him back on the bed. She fluffed her hair in the mirror and rushed out of her room. Sebastian followed.

Ariel ran down a flight of stairs but immediately stopped when she overheard Grimsby talking to Eric and another girl. The girl was named Vanessa, and she was beautiful. She had long, dark hair and was wearing a lovely blue dress and golden shell necklace. She hugged Eric and smiled.

Ariel hid behind a large column while she eavesdropped.

"It appears that I was mistaken," began a humble Grimsby. "This mystery maiden of yours does in fact exist."

Ariel was shocked.

Sebastian peeked through the banister and couldn't believe what he was hearing.

"And she is lovely," continued Grimsby, holding the maiden's hand. "Congratulations, my dear."

"We wish to be married as soon as possible," declared Eric.

Ariel shook her head in disbelief. She stayed hidden and breathed heavily.

"This afternoon, Grimsby," said Eric. "The wedding

ship departs at sunset." Eric was completely stone-faced. He didn't show a single emotion. He was still under a spell.

Ariel covered her face with her hands and began to cry. She ran away.

Vanessa looked over her shoulder and saw Ariel run off. She slyly rested her head on Eric's shoulder. She then gazed down at her shell necklace and quietly laughed to herself as the necklace began to glow.

Ursula's evil and twisted plan was unfolding perfectly. No one suspected that she was disguised as the young maiden about to marry Prince Eric—at least, not yet!

Chapter 24

Music played as the wedding ship left the dock. The ship was grand, with ornate details and beautiful wedding decorations. It was also filled with guests eager to witness Prince Eric's wedding.

Poor Ariel watched the ship from the dock and sighed. She slumped to the ground, dejected and heartbroken, sobbing with her head on her knees. She had no voice, and her dreams of being with Eric were crushed.

Sebastian sat beside Ariel, hanging his head in sadness. Flounder glumly floated in the water right below his sorrowful friends. Everyone was speechless—except Scuttle.

Scuttle happily flew through the sky humming a wedding tune. He headed toward the wedding ship out at sea for the perfect spot to view the nuptials. He was immediately distracted by a familiar female voice singing a song. He changed his path and flew down to a low porthole.

He peered through the window and saw a dark-haired maiden standing in front of a vanity, fluffing her hair. It was Vanessa, and she was wearing a white slip and the shell necklace. Her sweet voice was familiar to Scuttle, but her smile was very sinister. She danced on top of the vanity and turned the mirror toward her with a cackle.

Scuttle's jaw dropped. He was shocked by the reflection he saw in the mirror. "The sea witch!" he exclaimed. He backed away from the window frantically. "Oh no!" He flew as fast as he could back to the castle. "Ariel!" he called. "Ariel!"

He finally reached the dock and landed next to Ariel with a thump. He was exhausted and could hardly catch his breath. He tried to tell Ariel what he had seen, but his words became jumbled.

Sebastian listened impatiently while Ariel tried to figure out what Scuttle was saying.

"The witch was singing with a stolen set of pipes," he said finally. "Do you hear what I'm telling you?" Scuttle picked up Sebastian and shook him. He put the crab down and tried to speak a bit more coherently. "The prince is marrying the sea witch in disguise!"

Ariel gasped. It all made sense.

"What are we going to do?" asked Flounder.

Ariel realized she was running out of time. She had to kiss Eric before the sun set or she would turn back into a mermaid and become one of Ursula's slugs. Somehow, she had to make Eric see the truth. She dove off the dock and landed in the water next to Flounder. But without her mermaid tail, she could hardly swim. She began to flail in the water. She would never be able to swim after the ship!

Sebastian thought fast. He clipped a rope holding a bunch of barrels together on the dock. The rope and barrels fell into the water.

"Ariel, grab on to that!" yelled Sebastian pointing to the barrel. "Flounder, get her to that boat as fast as your fins can carry you."

"I'll try!" replied Flounder, grabbing the rope. He started swimming out to sea toward the wedding ship.

"I've got to get to the sea king," said Sebastian, standing on the dock next to Scuttle. "He must know about this!"

"What about me?" asked Scuttle, looking for a way to help.

"You find a way to stall that wedding!" yelled Sebastian as he dove into the water.

Scuttle thought for moment and came up with a perfect

plan. He flew full speed toward a swampy area filled with tall trees and squawked as loudly as he could. Small blue birds popped their heads out of wispy bushes and joined Sebastian in flight. Pink flamingoes stood up in unison and followed. Lobsters in the water heeded Scuttle's squawked battle cry. Dolphins and sea lions raced through the water.

"Move it. Let's go!" shouted a determined Scuttle. "We got an emergency here!"

The animals flew, swam, jumped, and sped toward the wedding ship. They heard Scuttle's message loud and clear—stall that wedding!

Back on the ship, the wedding guests bowed as Eric and his soon-to-be bride walked down a long, purple-carpeted aisle.

Vanessa wore a flowing white gown with a tight bodice and puffed long sleeves. A long veil draped down her back as she held a bouquet of beautiful red flowers. The shell necklace was her most prized accessory.

Eric walked stiffly beside his bride with a blank stare. The spell had completely put him in a daze. Max growled as the couple walked by—he knew Vanessa was not the right girl.

Eric and Vanessa stopped before an old minister, who

began the ceremony.

Meanwhile, Flounder was swimming feverishly toward the ship, pulling Ariel behind him.

"Don't worry, Ariel," said the tired but determined little fish. "We're going to make it! We're almost there!"

On the ship, the minister was reading the vows. Ursula, disguised as the maiden Vanessa, looked toward the setting sun and smirked. Then she glanced up at the hypnotized prince. She was only minutes away from victory.

"Do you, Eric, take Vanessa to be your lawfully wedded wife for as long as you both shall live?" asked the old minister.

"I do," replied Eric with a blank stare as his eyes glowed with magic.

Suddenly, Vanessa became distracted by a loud and obnoxious squawking. The sound got louder and louder. Within seconds, a flock of blue sparrows, led by Scuttle, zoomed over Vanessa's head. She ducked and angrily looked up at the birds, who were headed back in her direction. This time, they flew right under her wedding dress. Eric didn't even blink. He was unaffected by the pandemonium.

The birds feverishly flew all around the ship, causing the guests to run and scream in a panic.

Chaos ensued as sea lions hopped onto the boat.

Pelicans flew over Vanessa's head, dumping water in her face. Lobsters climbed on board and pulled her hair and snapped at her nose. Starfish stuck to her body and covered her mouth and face, and she let out a huge scream. A sea lion flipped Vanessa into the air with his big snout. Scuttle's plan was working!

Meanwhile, Flounder and Ariel finally made it to the ship. Ariel climbed up the side and over the railing. She saw the frenzied activity on the deck and watched Vanessa get tossed onto the giant wedding cake by a group of sea lions.

A group of dolphins jumped up from the sea and sprayed Vanessa with sea water. She was soaking wet, dripping with frosting, and red with anger.

It was Scuttle's turn to infuriate Vanessa. He let out a huge squawk in her ear. She grabbed him by the neck and shook him vigorously. Scuttle latched on to her shell necklace and pulled it with all his might. Vanessa tried to yank him off.

Max charged toward Vanessa and bit her backside. She let out a huge scream and finally let go of Scuttle. Scuttle pulled the necklace and the cord broke, sending the seashell flying through the air.

The seashell landed at Ariel's feet and shattered. The

golden vapor that held her voice was released. As the vapor swirled up and around her body, everyone heard the melody she had sung to Ursula when she signed the contract.

Instantly, Eric snapped out of his hypnotized state. The glow in his eyes was gone and he focused on Ariel. Grimsby and the wedding guests watched in shock as the golden vapor whirled around Ariel, while Vanessa angrily watched her plan dissolve.

The vapor and the melody reached Ariel's throat, and her voice returned! She held her neck and smiled. The sweet melody was coming out of her mouth!

"Ariel?" asked Eric.

"Eric!" exclaimed Ariel with a smile as Max jumped around her happily.

"You can talk!" declared Eric. He happily ran toward her. "You're the one!" He grabbed her hands and they stared longingly into each other's eyes.

"Eric! Get away from her!" shouted Vanessa in Ursula's voice. She was beginning to transform back into the evil sea witch.

"It was you all the time!" said Eric, wrapping his arms around Ariel.

"Oh, Eric, I wanted to tell you!" replied Ariel.

The two embraced as the sun met the horizon. They were just about to kiss when the sun set completely. Suddenly, Ariel lurched in pain and released her hold on Eric. She fell to the floor as her legs turned back into a tail. Eric watched helplessly.

"You're too late!" yelled the sea witch, laughing. She raised her arms to the sky victoriously, and bolts of lightning shot from her fingers. Her long, dark hair became short and gray, and her face once again became that of the evil Ursula. Her large, grotesque body bulged from the wedding dress as her tentacles burst out and covered the deck. Her beautiful disguise was gone.

The wedding guests gasped in horror!

Cackling, Ursula crawled across the deck and grabbed Ariel.

"So long, lover boy!" said Ursula as she dove into the sea with Ariel in her grasp.

"Ariel!" yelled Eric. He ran to the railing and watched the girl he loved slip away from him yet again.

Chapter 25

Ursula jerked Ariel underwater with Flotsam and Jetsam close behind.

"Poor little princess," began Ursula. "It's not you I'm after. I've a much bigger fish to—"

"Ursula, stop!" interrupted King Triton. The sea king stood before Ursula. He pointed his glowing trident at her face. Sebastian sat next to Triton's tail, glaring at the evil sea witch.

"Why, King Triton, how are you?" asked Ursula with a sly chuckle.

"Let her go!" demanded the king.

"Not a chance, Triton," replied Ursula angrily. "She's mine now! We made a deal." She magically made the contract appear. King Triton stared at Ariel's signature on the document.

"Daddy, I'm sorry!" yelled Ariel, trying to break free

from Flotsam and Jetsam. "I . . . I . . . I didn't mean to. I didn't know!"

Triton zapped the contract with his trident in hopes of breaking it to pieces. But the scroll remained intact.

"You see, the contract's legal, binding, and completely unbreakable, even for you!" declared Ursula with a smug smile.

Triton was shocked, discouraged, and worried. He lowered his trident, feeling utterly powerless.

"Of course, I always was a girl with an eye for a bargain," said Ursula, swimming around Triton. "The daughter of the great sea king is a very precious commodity!"

Swirls of lights from the contract engulfed Ariel in a golden cyclone. She began to shrink and change shape. She started to resemble one of Ursula's slugs.

"But I might be willing to make an exchange for someone even better," continued Ursula, taunting the king.

Triton stared at Ariel, horrified.

Meanwhile, Eric jumped off of the wedding ship and into a rowboat. He headed out into the ocean.

"Eric, what are you doing?" called Grimsby.

"Grim, I lost her once," began Eric, rowing with determination. "I'm not going to lose her again!"

Back in the sea, Ursula held the contract in front of Triton.

"Do we have a deal?" she asked.

If Triton signed the contract, Ariel would be free— and the king would take her place! It was exactly as Ursula planned from the very beginning. King Triton would belong to her, and she would rule the sea.

Triton was defeated. He had no choice. He had to save his daughter. He raised his trident and pointed it at the contract. With his head turned away, he signed and made the deal. Ariel's signature on the contract instantly changed to Triton's.

"It's done, then!" declared Ursula happily.

The golden cyclone around Ariel dissolved and she resumed her normal mermaid state. The cyclone then engulfed King Triton and transformed him into one of Ursula's slugs.

The witch cackled victoriously.

"No!" yelled Ariel upon seeing her father's altered body.

The once dignified and strong king was no bigger than Sebastian.

"At last, it's mine!" said Ursula, picking up Triton's crown and placing it on her head. She picked up the trident and watched it glow in her hands. Her newfound power made her gloat and giggle with joy.

Ariel leaned down next to her transformed father. She looked at Ursula and began to tremble with rage!

"You . . . you monster!" yelled Ariel, swimming up to Ursula and attacking her from behind.

Ursula threw Ariel to the ground and shoved the trident in her face but was distracted when a sharp object hit her in the arm. She turned around and saw Eric bobbing underwater. He had just thrown a harpoon at her!

"Little fool!" yelled Ursula. She ordered Flotsam and Jetsam to chase him.

"Eric, look out!" shouted Ariel.

Eric swam as fast as he could back up to the surface. He made it to his rowboat, took a deep breath, and tried to pull himself up. He was immediately dragged back down into the water by the evil eels.

Flotsam and Jetsam wrapped themselves around Eric and pulled him deeper into the ocean. He wouldn't be able to hold his breath for much longer.

Sebastian and Flounder watched as Eric struggled to escape. They dashed toward him to help him break free. Flounder slapped his tail across one of the eel's faces. Sebastian pinched the tail of the other eel with his claw. The eels winced in pain and let go of Eric, who frantically kicked back up to the surface.

Ursula was furious! She pointed her trident at Eric and blasted a bolt of magic at him in hopes of destroying him, but Ariel pulled on her hair and threw off her aim. Flotsam and Jetsam got zapped instead—and they disintegrated!

"Babies! My poor little poopsies," said Ursula, catching their remnants in her hands. She looked up and saw Ariel swimming after Eric. She was enraged. Her eyes became red. She breathed heavily and began to spout black ink from her tentacles. A plume of ink and smoke surrounded her as she grew larger and larger.

Sebastian and Flounder watched as Ursula became crazed with anger. There was no telling what she was capable of doing.

Chapter 26

Ariel and Eric swam to each other and embraced on the water's surface.

"Eric, you've gotta get away from here!" pleaded Ariel.

"I won't leave you!" replied Eric.

Suddenly, the water around them began to bubble and shake. Ursula's crown emerged from the water and rose between them. The sea witch was gigantic! Her head alone was as large as the wedding ship. Ariel and Eric hung from her crown like ornaments on a Christmas tree. She rose to the surface, and within seconds, her massive body floated on the sea.

Ariel and Eric dove off her crown and plummeted hundreds of feet before hitting the water. They gazed up at Ursula as she continued to grow even bigger.

"You pitiful, insignificant fools!" said Ursula, towering over Ariel and Eric. "You can't escape me!" She smashed a giant tentacle down, just missing them. "Now I am the ruler of all the ocean!"

Ursula created gigantic waves that carried Ariel and Eric away from each other. The sea was rough and angry and was no match for the couple. Ursula then used the trident to create a tremendous whirlpool. The whirlpool hit the bottom of the sea floor and stirred up all the debris lodged in the sand. An old and battered sunken ship rose to the surface, along with other boats and wreckage.

The ship was headed straight for Eric! He tried to avoid it but became submerged underneath it. Luckily, he managed to grab a rope attached to the ship. He pulled himself out of the water and up the side of the ship. He climbed over the rail and ran along the deck toward the steering wheel.

Meanwhile, Ariel clung to a rock. Ursula zapped the rock with the trident, sending Ariel flying into the air. She got tossed into the giant whirlpool and fell to the sandy sea bottom.

Ursula laughed and blasted at Ariel with the trident, narrowly missing her every time. The witch was so obsessed with her power that she didn't notice Eric driving a ship in her direction.

"So much for true love!" yelled Ursula as she prepared

to send one last blast down to Ariel.

Eric got closer to Ursula. A long, jagged mast projected from the front of the ship like a sword. At just the right moment, Eric turned the wheel. Ursula finally noticed the ship approaching her, but it was too late! Eric drove the ship right into Ursula! The sharp mast pierced her large body.

"Arrrghhhh!" screamed Ursula, her tentacles thrashing.

Eric jumped off the ship just as lightning struck, sending electricity coursing through the ship—and Ursula. The sea witch roared in pain. Bolts of lightning engulfed her body. She was dying, along with her magic. Her body began to disintegrate and she sank into the sea, dragging the ship down with her. Smoke filled the air as the water bubbled and boiled.

Eric swam to shore and collapsed in the sand.

Ursula's remains trickled down to her home under the sea. With the sea witch gone, the creatures in Ursula's garden instantly turned back into merfolk. Her evil spells were broken!

The trident fell to the sea floor and landed inches away from Triton. It glowed and instantly transformed him from a slug back into the king. He picked up the trident and held it proudly. He had regained control of the sea.

Chapter 27

The long and terrible night was over. The sun rose and lit the sky with pink and orange. The sea was finally calm. Lying on the sand, Eric began to awaken.

Unbeknownst to him, Ariel was sadly sitting on a rock in the sea, watching and wishing she were with him.

"She really does love him, doesn't she, Sebastian?" asked Triton staring at his unhappy daughter from a distance.

"Well, it's like I always say, Your Majesty," began Sebastian. "Children got to be free to lead their own lives." He giggled and shrugged.

King Triton sighed. He was about to make the most difficult decision of his life.

"Then I guess there's only one problem left," he said, looking seriously at Sebastian.

"And what's that, Your Majesty?" asked the crab.

"How much I'm going to miss her," replied Triton.

The king raised his trident and it began to glow. He aimed it toward the surface and a glowing vapor drifted through the water toward Ariel. It engulfed her tail, and her body began to sparkle.

Ariel looked down at her tail in amazement. It was transforming into legs! Ariel followed the trail of light back to her father out at sea. She gasped in excitement and gave him a radiant smile.

Triton and Sebastian smiled back at her.

Eric groggily began to sit up. He saw Ariel walking toward him. She was wearing a sparkling periwinkle gown. He smiled enthusiastically and ran to her. Then he picked her up and stared at her in awe. Ariel and Eric embraced and finally shared their first kiss.

Chapter 28

Wedding bells rang aboard a large ship adorned with painted images of mermaids on the bow. The deck was decorated with beautiful flowers and a purple and white canopy. It was a festive affair celebrating the marriage of Ariel and Eric.

Wedding guests clapped and cheered when the happy couple shared their first kiss as husband and wife.

Max excitedly jumped between Ariel and Eric and licked their faces. They smiled and patted him on the head.

Ariel's puffy-sleeved white gown was accented with a light green trim. Her golden tiara sparkled in the sun, and a long white veil flowed down her back.

Grimsby looked on proudly with Carlotta by his side. Carlotta could hardly contain her joy. Her lip quivered until she finally burst into happy tears. She used Grimsby's scarf to dry her eyes.

The sea was filled with merpeople floating on the surface. They waved to the newly married couple and the guests on the boat.

The happiest onlookers of all were the bride's father and sisters. They floated close together and waved to their beloved Ariel. Seeing her so happy filled their hearts with joy.

Scuttle lifted Flounder with his feet and flew him up to the ship to say goodbye to his best friend. Ariel gave Flounder a big kiss and patted Scuttle on the head. They waved as Scuttle lowered Flounder back down to the sea.

Sebastian sat teary-eyed on top of the giant white and pink wedding cake. He hugged the cake topper of Ariel and Eric. His joy quickly turned to fear as Louis the chef spotted him on the cake. Louis angrily chased Sebastian, but the quick little crab managed to outsmart the frantic chef. He cut a rope with his claw and released a pole that crashed into Louis's face, stopping him in his tracks.

Sebastian laughed triumphantly, then jumped off the boat and into the water.

Ariel walked to the side of the boat and leaned on the railing. She looked down at her father and smiled. King Triton gazed up at his youngest daughter. He magically created a wave that carried him up to the railing. Ariel gave her father a huge hug. She was so grateful that he had allowed her to follow her heart's desire.

"I love you, Daddy," Ariel whispered into her father's ear.

As the two released their embrace, Triton and Eric made eye contact. Eric smiled and bowed to the sea king. Triton returned the gesture and looked back at his daughter one last time. He rubbed her cheek and slowly lowered himself into the sea.

Ariel blew her father a kiss as her new husband joined her at the railing. Together, they waved goodbye to the merpeople.

Triton used his trident to create a magnificent rainbow. As the ship sailed farther out to sea, Ariel and Eric kissed— and they lived happily ever after.